LAST VENDETTA

EMMA LAST SERIES: BOOK TWO

MARY STONE

Copyright © 2023 by Mary Stone Publishing

All rights reserved.

No part of this book may be reproduced in any form or by any electronic or mechanical means, including information storage and retrieval systems, without written permission from the author, except for the use of brief quotations in a book review.

❦ Created with Vellum

This book is dedicated to those who have felt the weight of oppression and have had their voices silenced by unjust powers. May this dedication not only recognize your fight but also amplify it, carrying your story to hearts that will listen, minds that will understand, and hands that will act. You are seen, you are heard, you are worthy, and you are never alone.

DESCRIPTION

The wages of sin is death.

It sounds like a scene from a horror movie. But the carnage left by a literal axe murderer in the small town of Little Clementine is far too real.

Two families gruesomely slaughtered, two days apart, the only survivor a two-year-old girl.

The tight-knit community in the Allegheny Mountains is known for its religious fanaticism and aversion to the government. But without a police force, the sheriff has no choice but to begrudgingly accept the assistance of FBI's Washington, D.C. Violent Crimes Unit to solve the grisly case.

The brutality of the murders suggests the killer is one of the town's own—and these slayings were as personal as they were violent. But the residents of Little Clementine only take their problems to the Lord or their pastor, and neither are talking.

With no fingerprints, evidence, DNA, or leads, Special Agent Emma Last almost wishes for the appearance of the ghosts she can suddenly see to provide a clue. Because the murderer is the proverbial wolf in sheep's clothing, and the whole flock is in danger.

Last Vendetta, the second book in the riveting new FBI mystery series from bestselling author Mary Stone, peels back the veneer of small-town life to expose its terrifying underbelly. Brace yourself to confront the unsettling truth... while the Bible claims, "Vengeance is mine," there are those who disagree.

1

The henhouse door dragged over a puddle of broken ice, scraping away bits of knife-sharp shards as Rosemary Crawford nudged it shut. Whatever noise had awakened her hadn't come from the hens. They were sleeping soundly in their coop.

The iron latch came down snugly. Rosemary jiggled the door handle just to be sure. Waited. When no other sound but the January wind filled the night, she turned back to the house.

Only a few minutes earlier, Rosemary had been tucked into the rocking chair near her sleeping daughter's crib. She'd thought the strange squeaking was just her toddler kicking the crib slats again. But Ellie Sue had been dead to the world, her chubby lips smacking a dream bottle.

Rosemary remembered Old Man Tripp had seen a fox sneaking into his henhouse not a week ago. She'd grabbed a shawl and flashlight before heading out the door to check.

Everything seemed...fine.

But she couldn't shake the unsettling sensation.

You're acting like a paranoid old biddy. Stop it. You have decades to go before reaching "biddy" status. Stop it right now, before you drive your fool self crazy.

"I don't know what Ma and Pa would say to me right now." She pulled her shawl tighter around her shoulders and picked her way over the frosted grass, wishing spring would arrive already. "God protect me."

January in Maryland couldn't pass by fast enough.

Freezing temperatures were an exercise in patience under the best of circumstances. The cloudy night made everything worse, setting her off-kilter. She couldn't see the moon and stars like she normally could from the little homestead, and the air simply felt…well, wrong.

She smacked the side of her flashlight when it flickered not even halfway across the yard. "Just get me to the house, and I'll change your batteries, you stupid thing."

The screen door ahead of her screeched, and she nearly stumbled from surprise. A silhouette appeared on the back porch and brought her up short.

A second later, Rosemary's logic kicked in. "Chet, you scared the wonder outta…" Her words broke off as she shined the light up onto the porch in full.

It wasn't Chet.

Who is it?

Rosemary took another step forward, wishing more than ever for stars and moonlight. With only the little lamp above the door casting the silhouette and her dim flashlight offering scant illumination, the shadows disfigured her visitor's face. Halloween-ish, at best, whoever this person was. Rosemary felt sure she'd seen them in town, though. The set of the shoulders, the stance, and the step all struck her as familiar.

"Do I know you?"

"Oh, for sure you do, Rosemary. For sure you do."

The person's voice was like a rasp across the blade of a shovel—odd, ominous, and strangely masculine in nature.

With more bravado than she felt, Rosemary stepped forward. "It's late, and I need to be getting inside."

"Had to finally take care of something, Rosemary, that's all. How are you doing?"

She shook off the chill raising the hairs on the back of her neck and forced a laugh, thinking she might have recognized the voice at last. She opened her mouth to reply but froze with the words on her tongue.

Hanging from her visitor's hand was an axe…a bloody axe.

And now, watching the axe wielder descend the sagging steps, coat and overalls covered in blood, face obscured by an ill-fitting hat, Rosemary still wasn't certain of their identity or even their gender.

Or whose blood it was on that axe.

A flash of her daughter—sleeping, dreaming of a warm bottle of milk—shot through Rosemary's mind. She'd stepped out of Ellie Sue's room five minutes ago. That couldn't be Ellie Sue's blood.

It had to be—

Rosemary gasped.

The image was like a nightmare. Yet the axe-wielding figure seemed calm or under some kind of trance.

The ghoulish visitor reached the bottom of the stairs. Heavy, clipped steps crunched through the frosted grass, conveying every bit of confidence that had long since drained from Rosemary's heart.

"What in the name—"

"Shhh, Rosemary. Don't say anything, all right? I mean, you already know how to stay silent, don't you?"

"What have you done? *Tell me what you've done.*" The words took a ghostly shape as her hot breath met the icy air.

The unwelcome visitor inched another step in her direction.

"I took care of that abomination of a man, is all. Wiped him clean from the planet."

The person—*the murderer*, she knew now—swung the axe by their side, nonchalant, as they hummed a hymn.

"You killed Chet?" The amount of blood told the truth. Chet, the father of her child, was gone. She couldn't move or open her mouth to scream. She stood as rooted as the trees in the yard, witnessing evil approach her.

"Shhh."

"Where's Ellie Sue? If you laid one finger on her, I swear…"

They came closer, and Rosemary got a waft of her now-dead husband's tart, acidic blood. She gagged.

"You think I'd kill an innocent child? You think I'd hurt an innocent baby in her crib? You think I could do that?" Rage filled the axe wielder's voice, and the metallic scraping of the words now came like ice blown straight into Rosemary's ears.

She stumbled back and slipped on the icy ground. Her butt crashed onto the frosted grass. Her heart pounded.

"Just tell me you didn't hurt her," she whispered, choking on tears.

"A baby? You think I'm some kind of monster? How dare you! Rosemary Crawford, the Lord will judge you for this and all your sins."

The accusation stung, but in that moment, Rosemary had no voice, no power to defend herself. She thought only of Ellie Sue's safety.

Chet is gone. He's dead. I'm the only one standing between a murderer and Ellie Sue. Dear God, give me strength. Please, give me courage.

Rosemary lurched to her feet, charging her husband's

killer. She thrust her hands forward and shouted as the axe rose.

"I haven't committed any sins!"

The axe fell in a wide arc, shaving Rosemary's right shoulder. The dull ache of the hit was quickly replaced by searing agony. Hot blood cascaded down her arm. She staggered sideways, falling forward, but scrambled to her feet to get away.

She turned, facing her attacker, who took steady steps in her direction, lifting the bloodied axe again. Its blade now dripped with her and Chet's blood together.

As in life, so in death. If this is to be my time, I will join my husband in God's kingdom, knowing I did everything I could to protect our child.

"Silence in the face of evil is a sin."

Rosemary recognized the voice. "Then I'm not the only guilty one here."

"I know."

Clutching her injured arm, feeling light-headed from fear and the loss of blood, Rosemary stepped toward her attacker, ready to meet her fate.

"You'll be orphaning an innocent child." Maybe there was still some understanding behind those shadowed eyes. "Ellie Sue needs her mother."

For half a breath, Rosemary thought this tactic had worked.

The blade of the axe trembled, raised over the killer's head.

"Better an orphan than raised by sinners."

Rosemary bristled at the accusation. She staggered, half numb from the cold. "Get out of my way. I need to see my daughter!"

Her visitor sneered, their face a grotesque mask, covered in spatters of blood.

Rosemary rushed forward, thinking she could shove the lunatic aside, get to Ellie Sue's room, and lock the door. She'd just have to grab the phone in the hallway on her way so she could call the sheriff.

She could make it.

But when she met her attacker's eyes, Rosemary realized how wrong she was.

The axe came down in a violent chop, cleaving into Rosemary's neck. Blood and prayers abandoned her as the blade wrenched free from her flesh and came down a second and final time.

Not a sound slipped from Rosemary's mouth as she toppled sideways onto the dark, frost-coated earth, her final resting place.

2

Special Agent Emma Last willed her arms to stop trembling. But they seemed to have adopted a no-can-do attitude.

Her right palm was high in the air, her fingers splayed open as if she were drowning and reaching for help. Its desperate shadow shivered on the floor ahead of her. The grip her left hand had around her ankle might leave a bruise at this point. She felt ridiculous.

What the hell made me think yoga was a good idea?

"I can't even blame it on vodka." She muttered the comment to herself, but a nearby redhead giggled. Emma smiled.

At least someone thinks I'm funny.

Triangle pose appeared relatively easy until she'd attempted the maneuver herself. Now she knew she had all the flexibility of a stick pretzel.

There was no doubt in her mind that the handsome instructor, tilted over like a teapot at the front of the room, had been trying not to laugh since she'd begun.

"Remember, you're opening the chest and shoulders."

Oren spread his arms, breathing deeply. His muscles were lean and long, seeming to reach almost to the ceiling. He did not tremble at all. His eyes were also set on Emma.

"Make sure you're keeping your arms in a single, straight line, floor to ceiling." He paused, watching her with a quirked lip. She hated him a little bit but hated herself more for wanting to smile back. "If you feel you might topple, try adjusting the line of your feet to give yourself a bit more of a base."

If I adjust my feet in this pose, I'll start a domino train and knock us all down.

That was an exaggeration but not by much. Emma couldn't move. With her legs spread and her body strained into a geometric attempt at nirvana, she suspected she'd fall forward and break her nose if she budged a centimeter in any direction—or she'd fall over backward and break her tailbone. Her only alternative was to straight-up give up.

Emma Last does not give up.

Oren called for a transition, a *vinyasa*, ending in mountain pose—a simple standing position that Emma could actually handle.

Emma caught her breath during the brief interlude of standing like a real, live, normal human.

Then Oren lost all reason as he suggested the class try a headstand.

Covered in sweat, she ignored her shaking body in favor of studying her new instructor's inverted move, appreciating his physique. The man looked just as good upside down, maybe even better.

Apparently, Oren's figure and mad moves were a major draw at five thirty in the morning. Of the twenty attendees, Emma was the only beginner. The only one not balancing on her head, though she tried.

She might as well have had a spotlight shining on her ineptitude, but it was still no reason to quit.

By the time Emma twisted her body into the class's final pose, a manageable spinal twist on each side, the instructor caught her eye and nodded encouragement.

Message received. I'll hold the pose.

And she did, finally collapsing into *Savasana*, final resting pose.

When Emma sat up on her mat, half the other attendees were smiling and waving goodbye. The other half had surrounded Oren. She took a moment to flop back on her mat and close her eyes for another minute.

When she opened them, Oren Werling, the ridiculously good-looking instructor, stood directly above her in his loose yoga pants and overstretched, V-necked t-shirt. He'd somehow extricated himself from the throng of students.

"I'm Oren." He reached a hand down and pulled her to her feet. "And you are...?"

"Emma Last." She tightened her ponytail, suddenly self-conscious. "Thank you for the class. I feel like a clumsy chicken compared to your other students, but I guess that's what being a beginner is all about, huh?"

He chuckled, his blue eyes lighting up with amusement. "This is the beginners' class, so you're in good company. And I wouldn't call you clumsy or a chicken."

Easy there, Emma girl. He doesn't think you're a chicken. That's a good thing, right?

"So tell me, Emma Last. What got you interested in yoga?"

Well, you see, Oren, I'm trying to gain control over my interactions with dead people.

Nope, that probably wasn't the right thing to say.

Emma blurted out the most obvious thing she could think of that wasn't entirely a lie. "Uh, career stress?"

"And what is your career, if you don't mind my asking?"

"I'm a special agent for the FBI."

One of Oren's eyebrows rose nearly to his hairline. His blue eyes were shockingly bright and inquisitive. "Seriously?"

Heat flowed to Emma's cheeks. *One of these days, someone won't be surprised. Maybe.*

"It's true. I've been with the D.C. office for nearly two years now."

"Color me intrigued. I'd love to hear more, but I'm guessing that's classified."

A laugh escaped her throat—or had it been closer to a giggle?—and she shook her head, smoothing down her shirt over her hips. "We can talk while I put my shoes on. I'm still technically on my own time, so you don't need top-secret clearance to talk to me."

Oren's laugh was deliciously deep as he followed her over to the bench along the room's edge. "In all seriousness, I'm glad you found your way here. Yoga can be a fantastic way to gain self-mastery and manage stress. If you give the process some time, I believe you'll be pleased with the results."

She reached for her tennis shoes and sat back down, putting them on. "There've been a lot of changes around my office…and my life. And I've been meaning to try yoga for a while, so here I am. I may stand out, but I'll stick with it."

Lean and graceful, Oren folded himself down onto the floor mat a few steps from Emma. "Change is always difficult. And you may not have asked for it, but if you greet change as if you have, you can affect the transition and maybe gain some peace from your new circumstances."

Emma tightened her shoelaces, considering his words. "So you're essentially saying I should loosen up and be more open to change?" She'd meant the comment as a joke, but Oren seemed to see past the humor.

"Not at all. You seem very open. That's important for both the practice of yoga and life, so 'loosening up' wasn't what I had in mind. You did better keeping up with this crew than I would've expected of any beginner."

The compliment sent a flush of warmth through her chest. "Thank you. I appreciate that."

"You're welcome. I'm only saying that change happens. And a shift in circumstances of any kind is rarely comfortable. But if you actually work to choose the change as if you've asked for it rather than simply trying to accept what's happened, you may regain a sense of control." Oren stood in one fluid movement. "Do you want to stay for the next class? It's only a twenty-minute wait, and I promise to let you rest in between."

The sheen of sweat over Emma's chest and back grew chilly. A movement caught her attention at the other end of the studio. As she rose from the floor, she glanced past Oren...and did her best not to freeze. The last thing she wanted was for her new yoga instructor to think she was losing her mind.

An elderly man squatted in the corner of the studio. He seemed angry, his white eyes boring into her with an aggression that made her take a step back. As she prepared to turn away, the ghost actually growled at her.

The feeling's mutual, mister.

She could do without that old man—and every other ghost—just fine. If given the option.

Trying to refocus on the living man in front of her, Emma shook her head and picked up her coat. It was time to go. "I'm afraid not. I've got to get going, or I'll be late."

"But I'll see you again?"

The ghost dropped into a backbend. "Let's hope not. The Other doesn't want you, and I don't want you either. You're distracting my trainer."

Emma kept her eyes steady on Oren. No way was she going to look like a lunatic in front of him. She forced a wide grin and aimed her next comment at both Oren and the dead man. "You couldn't keep me away. I'll be back."

"*Ack-ugh.*" The ghost made choking sounds. "You're not good enough for him."

Oren, blissfully unaware of the heckling behind him, reached out and shook her hand. "It's a deal, and I'll look forward to it." With one last grin, he turned away and headed toward the lobby.

Emma allowed herself to watch him go.

What she'd said had been true. She had to get showered and head to work, to a morning riddled with paperwork since they'd wrapped up the Ruby Red Spectacle Circus case. But she also didn't want to wait around and allow the old yoga specter another opportunity to chitchat.

As Emma made the brisk walk to her apartment, her mind skirted toward what the circus's fortune teller had told her about a wolf, but she refused to consider Esther's exact words.

"The path to the wolf lies covered in innocent blood."

Whatever that meant, Emma was tired of being intimidated and threatened by the dead.

She'd been pestered by ghosts since becoming a special agent. First, a victim in Connecticut, Missy, appeared out of nowhere, warning Emma about "them" and saying, "They don't like you." Then Emma's friend and colleague, Miguel, offered cryptic warnings after being betrayed and murdered by his own team member. Two of her neighbors who recently passed had decided to stick around. One, Mrs. Kellerly, liked to bust into Emma's morning routine and advise her on how to make coffee. The other, Madeline Luse, would wave to Emma from across the courtyard, where she hovered on her family's balcony, watching her husband and their children eat dinner.

Emma had encountered no fewer than three gruesome

remnants of the murder victims in her last case, each of them no more helpful than a t-shirt that read, *I went to the circus, and all it got me was dead.*

It wasn't until she and her team had caught the killer that any of the ghosts actually spoke to her, offering confirmation for what she'd already learned.

Emma was exhausted by white-eyed dead people taking her by surprise, speaking in riddles, and generally making her life more of a horror show than it was to begin with. She'd joined the Bureau's Violent Crimes Unit to stop people who committed such crimes and to bring closure to any survivors.

Butting heads with ghosts wasn't supposed to be part of the deal. None of them had anything better to do than threaten and confuse her or—alternately—offer time-sucking small talk.

For the moment, a hot shower sounded positively magnificent.

3

Leo stood on his grandparents' front porch, gripping the railing so tight his hands ached from the strain. "Run, Papu, run!"

His lungs burned from screaming.

His grandfather should've been running to the house. He should've been escaping the pack of wolves just a few yards behind him. But Papu only trotted down the street.

The wolves howled, vicious and threatening, and Papu turned to look. Then he ran.

Leo's heart clenched as a wolf lunged and ripped a scrap off his grandfather's best khakis. The fabric hung from the creature's canines. Papu was a blur of desperation as he zigzagged around a tree. His silver-gray hair flashed under the glow of streetlamps. Leo wanted to run and help, but he couldn't even move.

Papu was too old for this. He couldn't possibly keep running.

Leo screamed again. "Papu, here! Run here!" He pounded the rail, trying to make enough noise to catch his beloved grandfather's attention.

The pack howled, growling and slobbering as they ran.

Leo panted, sucking in heavy gulps of air. The beasts were all *sizes now, from giant black-and-silver predators down to almost puppylike creatures in training.*

The wolf pack chased his grandfather along the street for what felt like an eternity.

Leo thought of his grandfather's gun cabinet. If he could get to it and retrieve the rifle, he would. But he didn't know the combination. Yaya, his grandmother, had always insisted children should not know how to unlock the gun cabinet until they turned sixteen.

Sixteen was six years away, and his grandfather was being chased now.

Tearing his gaze away from the scene in the street, Leo whirled back to the open door of his grandparents' home. "Yaya, help him! He's going to be killed!"

Just beyond the doorway, his grandmother lit her candles, making the sign of the cross. Unaware of—or uninterested in—her husband's impending doom.

"Yaya, the wolves are chasing Papu. Help! Call someone!"

The woman smiled over her candles.

Leo's lungs ached like they might burst.

He spun back toward the street to face the biggest of the wolves. And that was when its eyes—flat white with no pupils—found Leo.

A whimper escaped his lips, but he couldn't drive himself to retreat inside. His legs had frozen again, trapping him in this nightmarish standoff with a monster.

The wolf stalked forward, stopping just short of the porch steps. Its eyes, pale white, focused on him. Leo couldn't ignore the beast's gaze, even as the wolf bared its teeth and spoke in a gravelly voice that rumbled over him.

"The path to the wolf is covered in innocent blood."

"Yaya!" Leo Ambrose woke with a scream, jolting upright in bed.

Gasping, he stuffed a fist against his mouth, biting his knuckles to keep another scream from escaping.

His throat was raw, and he wondered how loud he'd been. How much he'd screamed in his sleep.

That blood. Fuck, that seemed so real.

Still panting, Leo sat up straight. He tried to count to ten, thinking he might shove the visage of that beast out of his mind if he could only calm his breathing.

"I'm in my house. In Washington, D.C. I'm thirty-one, not ten. I'm a fucking FBI special agent, and some giant fucking wolf did not eat Papu."

Papu died but not in the maw of a giant wolf with no pupils.

The darkness of his bedroom was brightened by a streetlight shining in dimly from one corner of the window. He was in his new house. Everything was okay. He was where he was supposed to be. After a few moments, his heart seemed like it might just stay in his chest after all.

Soaked in sweat, he centered himself. But the words of the wolf echoed in his mind.

"The path to the wolf is covered in innocent blood."

Rather than dwell on any doom-laden wolf symbolism, Leo swung his legs off the bed and shut off the alarm two seconds before it buzzed.

It was time for him to get up and get his ass to work.

He was an FBI agent, not a kid screaming for his grandmother's help against the big, bad wolf.

4

Maybe it was the yoga afterglow, or perhaps the Oren afterglow, but the Violent Crimes Unit felt surprisingly cheery for a Monday morning. Emma leaned back in her chair and sipped some more coffee, enjoying the banter and good moods of her fellow agents as they all compared weekends and traded stories. With only one case under their belts as a new team, bonding was welcome and even essential.

Emma couldn't imagine a better way to start a workweek. She'd so enjoyed her time with Mr. Oren Werling that even the ghostly yogi in the corner hadn't ruined her mood.

Even Leo's normal intensity was dialed back. "...then the car, which Jeff had left in neutral, started rolling down the hill—"

"No!" Special Agent Denae Monroe spit out her coffee, choking on laughter.

Leo pressed on with his high school hijinks. "So Jeff as Batman and me as Superman are chasing this car, trying to stop it, and the whole cheerleading squad starts this whole cheer—"

"No, they didn't." Emma chuckled.

The anecdote fit Agent Leo Ambrose to a T. Talk about someone with a superhero complex.

Emma still missed her former teammate Keaton Holland and SSA Neil Forrester like crazy. But at least she had new teammates around her, and the old ones no longer felt like phantom limbs.

It'll be okay, Emma girl. Choose the change, remember? And you've got plenty of entertainment in the meantime.

She hid another small chuckle behind her coffee cup.

"I have a small confession." Special Agent Mia Logan, at the next desk over, still smiled from Leo's story. As she set down her coffee cup, a soft blush came over her cheeks, which told Emma the subject was about to change.

Denae Monroe, always one for confessions and gossip, encouraged Mia from across the room, beckoning with her hand like she wouldn't miss this for the world. "Tell, tell."

"Vance and I went out this weekend."

Emma glanced over at fellow agent Vance Jessup. His clean-cut face told no tales, which didn't discourage Denae in the slightest.

Denae fluttered a napkin in front of her body in an exaggerated fanning motion.

"It's no big deal, but I thought I should mention it...if anything came up." Mia straightened her back, clearly trying to keep her dignity.

Denae leaned forward. "And did...*ahem*...anything come up?"

Vance wadded up a piece of scrap paper and threw it at Denae.

Emma was about to call a halt to Denae's antics when the VCU's main door burst open.

SSA Jacinda Hollingsworth's grim expression drained the smiles from everyone's faces.

"Team, we have a literal axe-murderer situation in a tiny Maryland town called Little Clementine." Jacinda pocketed her phone and pulled her wavy red hair into a bun.

Emma was quickly learning that whenever the SSA pulled her hair back, it meant business.

"Shit," Leo muttered.

"The town's nestled in the Allegheny Mountains, and there's no police force. The local sheriff has requested we take over the case, and I've agreed."

Denae stood, already picking up her coat from where she'd draped it over the back of her chair. "How many dead?"

"Two families killed, two days apart. Four dead total. The only survivor is a toddler."

Mia gasped, and Emma was dimly aware of Vance setting a hand on her shoulder.

Four dead in two days was one hell of a spree.

Jacinda waved them all toward the door. "Come on and get a move on. You've got forty-five minutes to gather whatever you need and get back here. I hope your go bags are packed. We'll be staying in Little Clementine until further notice. I'll hold a phone conference on the two-hour drive and get everyone up to speed. Prepare yourselves. It's gruesome."

On that note, the supervisory special agent skirted by the central desks and headed toward her office, leaving Emma and the others to scatter.

Although she was still adjusting to Jacinda's on-the-go briefings, they were something of a welcome change...one she could absolutely embrace.

SSA Neil Forrester had never allowed his team to step foot out of the VCU's main office until they'd combed through every detail of a case. She'd had to practically sit on her own hands during many of his briefings to keep herself from running out the door.

Much as she missed SSA Forrester, Jacinda's style suited Emma's nature better, if she was honest with herself.

Emma grabbed her keys and her coat for the quick run home to pick up her go bag. She could've kicked herself for taking the bag out of her car. She'd refreshed it a couple of weeks back but hadn't returned it to its rightful place.

As they passed through the lobby downstairs, Denae slid her arm through Emma's. "Do you think Jacinda meant a literal axe murderer? Maybe the sheriff got the details wrong?"

Emma shook her head as they headed into the parking lot. "No idea, but even if they mistook the murder weapon for an axe, with four people dead, it has to be bad."

Denae skidded to a stop beside her new dark-blue Ford Escape, parked just beside Emma's Prius. "Agreed. See you in a few."

Emma slammed her driver's side door and started the car. The day, which had seemed so cheery only thirty minutes before, was now somber.

Back at her complex, Emma raced up the stairs to her apartment. Heading to her closet, she noted that her mother's picture remained upright.

I'm actually disappointed.

A little echo of longing hit her, slowing her movements.

Despite the rushed time frame, Emma stared at her nightstand for another second, waiting to see if the frame would fall over in front of her. She liked to think the picture's constant tumbling was her mother's way of letting her know she wasn't alone.

Gina Marie Last never appeared to Emma the way every other ghost did.

Emma thought again of what Oren suggested. Maybe she should choose the changes as something she'd asked for. She determined to give the method a serious try.

With her go bag over her shoulder, Emma turned from her room and shut the door firmly in her wake. She sped off so she wouldn't be tempted to turn around to see if the photo fell.

She had an axe murderer to catch.

5

Leo gave in to his baser instincts and grabbed the "oh shit" handle above the Expedition's passenger door, trying to look casual and probably failing.

Emma's driving left something to be desired when it came to passenger safety. Now that she'd merged onto the Beltway surrounding D.C. proper, there was no slowing her down.

He swallowed against a lump in his throat. Anything resembling reckless driving made him nervous. His parents had died in a car wreck—a harsh lesson that had taught him to be cautious. At least the weather was clear.

Maybe she's just testing me?

There was always a bit of hazing when joining a new team.

Then again, maybe she was just a lunatic driver.

Emma squeezed their oversize vehicle between two sedans in the middle lane, and he retracted the hazing option. A woman who knew how to drive like this—without getting killed—wouldn't use her skill behind the wheel as a form of hazing.

This was just the way Emma drove, like a hellcat with a hellhound nipping at her tail.

He forced a smile, trying to portray a devil-may-care attitude. "Beltway traffic, huh?" Without waiting for an answer, Leo distracted himself by opening his iPad. "Jacinda should call any minute."

Emma grunted in response, swerving into the fast lane and roaring past a minivan.

Feeling more comfortable with Special Agent Emma Last after their last case, he'd chosen to ride with her. Like an idiot. To his knowledge, Emma was a perfectly reasonable human being. But her lead foot triggered his fight-or-flight response.

Between last night's dream of wolves attacking his grandfather and the company of Emma the Speed Demon, stress was becoming his constant companion.

Joking with his new team this morning had been exhausting. He'd been trying to keep the wolf nightmare at bay. Seeing the smiles had relaxed him a bit, but he'd been faking his damn face off.

SSA Hollingsworth appeared at an angle on his screen. But Leo had to look away, dizzy from the swaying and the momentum of the Expedition.

"Here she is."

Emma grunted again in response, quick-shifted back into the middle lane before merging into the right lane, taking the lead in their small caravan.

Leo positioned his iPad so that Emma, his lunatic chauffeur, wouldn't be distracted by the screen.

Jacinda's expression was serious, and her face was close to the camera. "Everyone hear me?"

"Loud and clear." Leo shifted sideways to show Emma beside him. "Agents Last and Ambrose present and accounted for."

Vance echoed in the affirmative from where he drove with Mia. Denae drove Jacinda, which made their team complete.

Bet we'll get there an hour ahead of everyone else.

"Good. Listen up." Jacinda cleared her throat, and some emails popped up on Leo's screen to show exactly what she was typing.

Case files, check.

"Two nights ago, an unknown assailant entered the home of Ernie Murray, white male, age forty-six, and Louise Murray, white female, age forty-four. The assailant used a hatchet or an axe...murder weapon is still being determined...and slaughtered them in their sleep. There was no apparent struggle. Forensics didn't find fingerprints, footprints, trace evidence, or DNA. Open the first set of pictures I sent. You should have both victims' pictures to view."

Leo clicked on the first photo, revealing a close-up of a grisly beheading. Or...all but.

The killer had swung their weapon with enough force that a fairly clean blow had nearly severed Ernie Murray's head. A small strip of skin and muscle remained, attaching the head to the body. The victim's eyes were closed. Blood, thick and caked, hid whatever his hair color might have been. Muscle and bone could be seen in the image, from the neck and head both. Leo wished the photos were in black and white.

Emma looked over to see what he was viewing. The Expedition swerved right. She turned her focus back to the highway—a move Leo was grateful for. "Yikes. Talk about a glamour shot gone wrong."

Leo swallowed bile back down his throat and opened the next photo.

The full-body shot of Ernie Murray revealed the killer

had gotten their exercise on that victim. The man had been left in pieces. "A lot of rage here. Look at this."

Emma glanced sideways fast just before womanhandling the Expedition into an exit lane. "Oh shit. What is that? Half a dozen strikes?"

Leo shifted his focus to the notes. He wondered whether the fluttering in his gut was more from the photos or Emma's driving. "Close. Scene notes suggest eight strikes of an axe or axe-like weapon."

"Next image…" Jacinda's instruction was somber.

Louise Murray was spared the overkill level of anger her husband had attracted. She'd been beheaded, just like him, but her body showed no other signs of attack. Her arms and legs were flat and extended. If it weren't for the blood and missing head, she appeared to be at peace.

Leo turned his attention away from the photos. Jacinda's patient expression stared out of the screen, giving all of them time to process.

"Wonder if they saw it coming?" He'd spoken under his breath.

Emma slowed the vehicle just a touch, showing a bit of mercy. "I hope they were sleeping. Seeing an axe heading toward you, inescapable…I don't even want to think about it."

Leo's mind flashed to the slobbering wolf from his dreams, its muzzle getting closer, and imagined the feeling of dread had been similar for the victims. Or worse.

Jacinda's voice stole him away from that question, thankfully.

"All right, team, you've seen the aftermath from the first set of victims. Here are the basics. The Murrays' hog farm is far removed from neighbors' eyes and ears. An anonymous call to the station in Zeigler City…the county seat…alerted the sheriff's department to the crime. Sheriff Larry Lowell, who'll meet us in Little Clementine, handled the scene. His forensic team documented everything and took the bodies to the morgue at the county seat. The local preacher, Pastor Gregory Darl, is as close to a town mayor as Little Clementine's got, and to the sheriff's way of thinking, he was the most logical person to contact initially."

Mia interrupted. "The Murrays didn't have other family?"

"No known family in the area." Jacinda shook her head. "But they were well known. Faithful parishioners, it seems. Pastor Darl requested the sheriff keep the murders quiet until law enforcement had some answers for his congregation so as not to cause a panic. The sheriff agreed, thinking it was an isolated incident. But we're talking about a town with forty-seven citizens suddenly cut down to forty-five, and that was before the second couple was found. Population forty-five, now down to forty-three."

Vance spoke up. "That had to hit them hard, unless they're the kind of rural community with miles between every homestead. What do we know about this place?"

"Sadly, not very much, and that's partly by design. Little Clementine is a small community, with most homes in walking distance of others or central meeting places. They're a tight-knit bunch known for their religious zeal and distaste for government."

"Religious extremists?"

"We don't know much beyond what the sheriff's told us, so I'm hesitant to use the word 'extremist' yet. But they are definitely a conservative Evangelical sect. Not what you find in D.C., and from what we can tell, they'd have preferred to keep it quiet."

"Unbelievable," Emma muttered.

Jacinda tapped at her tablet. "But last night, the 'keep it quiet' plan went down the tubes. Another family, this one with a chicken farm closer to town, was targeted. Files incoming."

Leo noted the icons that popped up below Jacinda's image but kept his eyes on the SSA. After seeing Louise and Ernie Murray's final state, he was in no hurry to view the next set of crime-scene photos.

"Second verse, same as the first. Chet and Rosemary Crawford were hacked apart just like the first couple. A few notable differences. One, while Chet was killed in his bed, his wife was in the front yard when she was attacked, presumably coming back from their chicken coop. So positioning. Second difference, the Crawfords had a two-year-old daughter named Ellie Sue. She was spared. It's unclear, however, whether leaving her alive was an oversight or an actual mercy."

Leo tapped the Raise Hand icon, drawing Jacinda's attention. She nodded. "The first couple, the Murrays, had no children? None who might've been out for the night?"

"No, they were childless." Jacinda squinted, reviewing some more information before continuing. "Third difference, the Crawfords have local family. Ellie Sue Crawford, the toddler, is now staying with her grandparents, Rosemary Crawford's parents. Bishop...that's his name, not a station... and Cora Hardy."

Leo opened a picture of the little girl. She was a cute kid. He turned the screen so Emma could glance at it.

"Poor baby," she murmured.

Jacinda scrolled, reading more details. "Fourth difference, there was no anonymous call. A neighbor and his young son spotted Rosemary Crawford's remains in the yard while driving by early this morning. The pair were cleared of any wrongdoing by officers."

Denae spoke up. "But it's a small town, so you can bet

everyone in town knew everything about the murders within minutes."

Jacinda nodded. "Exactly. I'll leave you to review the second set of images after we get off this call, but you'll get déjà vu. They're so similar. Sheriff Lowell has set up a base for us at the community's church for lack of any other suitable place. That's the address in your GPS units now. On the way, review the details and get your brains working. We'll discuss theories and game plans when we meet with the sheriff. Any questions?"

Leo could only shake his head.

When everyone signed off, he opened the second set of photos. Mentally, he added one more difference from the last couple to those Jacinda had noted.

Whereas the last couple had looked to be about the same age, Chet Crawford had been noticeably older than his wife.

Even with their faces covered in blood, the age difference was easy to see. He confirmed from the notes.

Chet Crawford, white male, forty-eight.

Rosemary Hardy Crawford, white female, twenty-six.

Chet had been just over two decades older than his wife.

Emma glanced at the photos before taking a sharp left. "Like Jacinda said. Second verse, same as the first."

In an echo of Emma's earlier responses, Leo let out a noncommittal grunt.

Words had left him.

Little Clementine's religious nature niggled at him. It felt extreme, even though Jacinda had avoided using that word. He thought of Yaya's never-ending prayers and candles. Although he'd certainly never suffered any abuse from the Church as a kid, he'd walked away with no fond memories.

Not that I'd let Yaya know that.

He fought back the urge to reach for his Saint Jude medal. Yaya had given him the token when she learned he was joining the FBI. Saint Jude was the patron saint of lost causes. Yaya wanted to make sure he remembered his work did not define him. He might be forced to confront people who were lost causes, but he should never become such a person himself. Leo understood law enforcement carried a risk of becoming traumatized, and that sometimes agents or officers would find themselves leaning over the abyss. But he wouldn't allow himself to slip. He couldn't. And because he loved his grandmother, he wore the medal.

But this wasn't a case where he wanted to appear religious…at least, not unless it suited his needs in interviewing townspeople.

On top of everything else, they were setting up base in a church, of all places.

He could only imagine how the thought would scandalize his grandmother, murders or not.

"A church is a place of prayer and reflection. Lower your voice. Humble yourself."

How many times had he heard those words…

No, he would've preferred meeting anywhere else, for a whole multitude of reasons.

A shudder ran through him. He was surprised how strongly he was responding to the idea of what his team was embarking on.

He caught Emma taking a suspicious peek. Reading him.

Great. Here's hoping Yaya lit a candle for me over the weekend.

6

I sat with my legs hanging free over the cliff's edge. The peace of this blessed perch did little to calm me, however. Whenever I needed to clear my head or speak to my Lord… this was the place where I sought refuge in His great landscape above my town.

It offered me no refuge this morning.

Only loneliness greeted me in the dawn's light. Sorrow created a hollowness in my center. I took a deep breath, filling myself as best I could with the Lord's creation. But even the very air grated against my throat, scratchy and hoarse from all my crying.

Steadying myself, I let my breathing settle and forced the sobs back down.

"The *Lord* is my strength and song and is become my salvation. The voice of rejoicing and salvation is in the tabernacles of the righteous: the right hand of the *Lord* doeth valiantly." The words rang hollow from my throat, though I'd repeated Psalms 118:14-15 from my handy King James, and others, since coming to the clifftop.

I was exhausted. My shoulders ached from hefting the

axe. Last night, as I'd lifted and lowered the weapon, it had been no heavier than my own arm. No weight burdened me in the throes of delivering righteous justice.

Seeing Chet Crawford sleeping so peacefully caused rage to burble in my throat. He'd almost looked innocent.

Chet Crawford, a man many years older than his wife.

A man's man.

He hadn't seen the axe coming. One swift hack to end the evil of Chet Crawford.

A hawk climbed higher in the sky, coming up toward the clifftop from the trees. It veered sideways upon seeing me. I didn't blame God's creature. He must've sensed the darkness in me. The hate that had burrowed into my soul.

I'd killed Chet and his wife swiftly, though. Delivering Rosemary from this earthly plane had been a good thing. If Rosemary Crawford knew her husband's proclivities and allowed them to continue, she was just as culpable. Silence was complicity. *It is our duty to stop evil where we see it.* I was ashamed of how long I'd waited to extinguish the evil lurking in our Lord's town.

But better late than never.

Beneath me, rocks shifted. I held tighter, anchoring myself to God's ground. In His plan.

Rosemary, the mother of sweet Ellie Sue—only two years old and now orphaned. But I meant what I'd said.

Better an orphan than raised by sinners.

"No. I'm carrying out the Lord's plan, delivering evil from the land." I inhaled God's freshest air. Centering myself on the trees in the distance, I focused on the words of 1 Samuel 16:7, reciting them by heart.

"But the Lord said unto Samuel, Look not on his countenance, or on the height of his stature; because I have refused him: for the *Lord* seeth not as man seeth; for man looketh on the outward appearance, but the *Lord* looketh on the heart."

That's right. The Lord seeth His plan and my matching intentions. That is what matters.

Beads of sweat collected on my brow despite the cold of the morning. I knew I was in the right, but making a stand now was still a difficult step for me.

Chet Crawford had been evil. "Ripe for reaping rather than redemption," as the old pastor might have said. I'd kept going after that first hack because he deserved so much more than a single death blow.

And then Rosemary, who I'd assumed was with the baby, hadn't been in the house at all.

No, she'd been outside with the chickens she doted over.

The Lord must know that I was righteous, but the pain I experienced was absolute. Regardless of God's plan, I'd also done evil.

Is it evil if a sin is in service to His plan? Can it be?

Kicking my heels against the cliff face, I gnawed at the question.

Until she'd mentioned Ellie Sue, I'd been trying to figure out a way to spare Rosemary. But the way she looked at me—like I might have actually murdered a baby. The rage that had dropped over me was all-consuming...I'd never known anything like it. How dare she!

I wasn't a monster. I simply wasn't.

I am a messenger.

Chipmunks chittered from the trees beside me, reacting to some predator. But they seemed to chuckle at me. Making fun of my pain. Mocking my regret.

But anyone would've lost their mind like I had.

Rosemary stared at me like I was the Devil himself...

Yet she'd been in league with the evil of our town. She'd married it, laid with it, and exposed her daughter to it.

I might have made an orphan of Ellie Sue, but I'd saved her from far worse a fate.

My heels ached now, the way I was hitting them against the cliff face, but I kicked harder, relishing the pain as tears erupted in my eyes. Again.

Even the hawk saw me as evil and veered away.

"God, give me strength. Help me, oh Lord…" The aching loneliness returned. My own sins weighed heavy on me. I'd brought this loneliness upon myself.

Tears burned my tired eyes. Much as I rubbed, teardrops came faster and harder until I gave in, shaking and weeping and coughing out my prayers in supplication. I hoped God heard me.

You must hear me. Do you?

"God, God…give me strength…to finish what I've started…in service to your plan, God…and forgiveness… forgiveness," I coughed, "for what I've done. I am not a monster. *I am not a monster.*"

The sun continued glaring at me, burning its sight into me, but it brought no warmth. I shivered in the icy stare of its glory. The sun was a sign, I knew. God did still see me. He did still believe in me. Me, enacting his plan for all our town to see.

"Lord, give me strength. Amen."

I evened my breath, fighting more tears. There was no time for them.

The Lord's plan needed delivering.

I wasn't done yet.

There were others to bring to justice before I could rest.

7

The Jubilant Ridge House of Faith wasn't much to look at. The old lodge-style church sat on a small rise of land near the two-lane state road, which served as the main thoroughfare for Little Clementine. On the way to the church, the FBI caravan of black Expeditions passed the town's best excuse for a bodega, with an attached gas station. The next and final block of Little Clementine's main drag boasted a combined hardware and general store and a tiny two-story motel with a faded sign that read, *Heights of Glory Inn*.

"Not quite the tourist hot spot, is it?" Emma had seen small towns before but wondered how this one qualified as more than a dot on the map.

"Not quite any kind of *spot*, is it?" Leo had finally removed his fist from around the "oh shit" handle twenty miles back and seemed fairly relaxed. "But there are people."

The whole town—and all its forty-three citizens—seemed to have gathered outside the church. Emma drove a block past the structure and idled on a dirt side road to wait for the slower drivers in their party to catch up.

"Not going in?"

She shook her head. "Jacinda's in charge. Let her handle that crowd."

After about fifteen minutes, the other two vehicles appeared. Emma pulled into the church's gravel lot at the end of the caravan.

All eyes turned to the three badass Expeditions. Surrounded by broken-down sedans and pickups, their party couldn't have looked more out of place if they'd tried.

Emma killed the engine. She tugged her bag from the back seat and caught Leo's gaze. "Ready to be the center of attention?"

The agent grinned. "Always."

Emma spotted the squint around his eyes, suggesting he was lying, but didn't call him out on it. Leo had been strangely subdued during the ride. She chalked it up to the gruesome images but sensed there might be an extra layer to his thoughtfulness. Twice, she'd noticed him shifting his pendant under his shirt, as if it irritated him.

Without offering more of a clue to his thoughts, Leo opened the door and hopped out, leaving Emma to follow suit.

Emma gathered with her team in front of the SUVs, eyeing the small crowd between them and the church. Some three dozen or so adults and teens stood ahead of them, their expressions ranging from defensive to sorrowful.

As if they'd been told to form some sort of grim wedding ceremony, the townspeople split, leaving a path through their midst to the front of the church.

Emma felt surrounded. There was no other word for it.

Two men exited the church and walked down the middle of the aisle toward the agents. Neither one seemed aware of the scene's performative aspect.

The man in uniform was clearly the sheriff, so Emma

focused on the other. "Must be the pastor here." She'd spoken out of the corner of her mouth, but Jacinda nodded.

Pastor Gregory Darl was tall and slim, with reddish-brown hair and a formal gait, suggesting he was used to leading the way. In a dark, well-fitting suit, he was by far the most formally dressed of anyone present.

Emma pulled at her white cotton blouse, wrinkled from the drive.

On Jacinda's other side, Agent Denae Monroe coughed, perhaps to hide a chuckle. "Is that a Bible under his arm?"

Jacinda hissed at her to hush. "The church is central to this community, Agent Monroe. So get used to seeing Bibles. He's the leader of this parish. Let's see what he says, how he presents himself. Better to get the lay of the land now. I don't want to handcuff a mob on the first day. My superiors might start to think it's a trend."

Emma had to hide a snicker. Only a week back, the team had been attacked by a local angry mob in the middle of a circus. Their weapon of choice was ketchup, but still.

Throughout the formal introductions, Emma kept her eyes on the crowd. On either side of her, Jacinda and Leo stood like soldiers. Jacinda was in charge, which accounted for her stiff stature and manner. Leo's tension was still an intriguing puzzle for the moment.

"Welcome to Little Clementine. I'm Sheriff Lowell." The sheriff shook Jacinda's hand and nodded to the rest of them. Then he turned and led the way toward the church, nodding to townsfolk as he directed the agents inside. "I'm going to take you down to the church basement, where Pastor Darl has set up some space for you as best he could."

"It's where we hold potlucks, wedding receptions, family reunions…community events." The pastor's voice held a pride that wasn't quite matched by the doom and gloom radiating from his congregation. He kept talking as he led them inside.

Emma tuned out his impromptu history of the church in favor of taking the building in for herself.

The space was warm, despite the cold outside. The building was solid and well taken care of. The front doors opened into the main chamber lined with caramel-colored wooden pews that made her butt hurt just looking at them. A pulpit dominated the front of the space. Wavy window glass caught and reflected the early afternoon sun throughout the interior.

The pastor led them to a set of stairs set into a small alcove.

It doesn't smell like a church.

Though she had no idea what a church *should* smell like, that was her first thought. In her limited experience, they tended to smell like incense and dying flowers.

This space smelled like…a nonentity. Dry wood and old paint.

Following her team down the shadowed stairwell, Emma found herself in a large, semifinished basement space. Concrete walls, painted the same dull white as upstairs, made the place appear sterile. Low ceilings gave her a sense of claustrophobia. The carpet was thin. Emma felt the chill from the concrete floor beneath it.

Hard to believe they have friggin' wedding receptions down here. Where the hell do they find the joy?

At the edge of their group, Agent Mia Logan hugged her arms around her chest as if to ward off a chill. Emma didn't blame her. There was no comfort to be found in the space.

A folding banquet table, stained with years of coffee or maybe punch, stood off to the side. Folding chairs had been set around it.

"If y'all will join me over here." The sheriff led them into the far corner of the basement. "I'll go over what we've got so far."

To Emma's surprise, the sheriff allowed the pastor to join the group heading to the briefing area. Even from across the room, she saw an old-fashioned chalkboard with bloody crime-scene photos taped up. Law enforcement officers permitting civilians to see the murder board was not typical procedure.

"Sheriff? Are you sure you want the pastor to be part of this discussion? This could compromise the case." SSA Hollingsworth glanced between the sheriff and the pastor in quick succession.

"As the leader of this town, as its spiritual beacon, I am no compromise to your investigation. I am, if anything, more invested in finding this devil than you." Pastor Darl stood rooted to the basement floor, daring Jacinda to move him.

"Be that as it may, Pastor, I can't encourage your presence. We have your town's best interest at heart—"

"I am the town's heart, its soul—"

Sheriff Lowell stepped between the pastor and the SSA, cutting off whatever Pastor Darl was about to say. "I fully understand your position, SSA Hollingsworth, and I agree with you. But..." He held up a hand to keep the pastor quiet. "I'm afraid the horses are out of the barn. Pastor Darl has seen our investigation so far, and I believe he can be a valuable consultant."

Jacinda's nostrils flared. "But—"

"I'm the one who will have to deal with the D.A." Lowell tapped his chest. "I believe listening to Pastor Darl will give you a...more thorough understanding of the community."

Stopped the fight right when it was getting good.

The pastor had only said a few words so far, but he already grated on Emma's nerves. She'd been looking forward to Jacinda ripping into him.

Jacinda was never one to dare.

For a moment, Emma thought she would get her wish anyway. Jacinda's eyes narrowed. But the SSA seemed to catch Lowell's implied meaning. Pastor Gregory Darl and his attitude would be very telling about the town of Little Clementine. They needed to observe him.

Jacinda acquiesced. "Fine. But I reserve the right to remove him if necessary."

"Absolutely," the sheriff agreed before the pastor could protest further.

"Then, let's get to work."

Emma looked away from the bloody crime-scene photos as she sat down in a folding chair, peering into the corners of the room. Since this was a church, she'd prepared herself for a fair number of white-eyed dead people.

So far, she hadn't seen a single ghost.

Didn't the town hold funerals here? Where else but in their church? Shouldn't there have been ghosts observing this little get-together?

"Autopsies are currently being performed on the victims." Sheriff Lowell ranged his hand along the pictures. "But as you can see, cause of death appears more than clear. Strangely, the last person to see any of our victims alive was the church photographer, a Mr. Wade Somerson, who's been putting together a community directory. The man doesn't have an alibi—"

"He's a widower." Pastor Gregory Darl stepped forward. "And lives alone, but you should trust him as you would me."

Emma barely kept a straight face. *We don't know if we should trust* you *yet, Pastor.*

Pastor Darl remained oblivious to any questions of his trustworthiness, though, and kept going, all but pushing the sheriff to the side as he moved in front of their seated group. "I've known Wade Somerson since childhood. He's a plumber who works as the church handyman and our community's photographer. This congregation is his life."

The sheriff placed a hand on the pastor's shoulder to quiet him. Sheriff Lowell directed his next words at the community leader rather than the federal agents. "As unlikely a suspect as he may be, they'll want to speak to him."

"He's right." Jacinda stood, facing the two men. She offered a disarming smile. "And as small as this community is, unlikely suspects don't exist in cases like this. Nobody wants to believe that anyone, especially anyone they know, is capable of…this sort of crime."

Delicately finished.

Emma rose and approached the makeshift crime board. When she came within reach of the photos, she pointed to the men's bodies. The first two victims, the Murrays, were pictured directly above the third and fourth victims, the Crawfords. Since the pastor had already seen what there was to see, she saw no point in sugarcoating things.

"Pastor, Sheriff…the extra time required for this level of brutality suggests there's something personal between these victims and the killer. The men's bodies are all but eviscerated. This murderer knew these victims and had animosity toward the men in particular."

"He killed the women too!" The pastor's voice rose so high that it echoed.

Emma let the words die in the air before she traded glances with Jacinda, who gestured for her to go on.

"Obviously, we have four victims here who suffered." Readjusting the focus she'd brought to the photos, Emma stepped in front of the board, blocking the pastor's view of the bodies. "But there was more ill feeling toward the men. The number of blows indicate that."

She hesitated before continuing, but Jacinda nodded encouragement. "And considering all our victims were faithful parishioners, moving through the same circles, it's also probable that someone involved in the church is responsible."

The pastor's face grew redder and redder as Emma spoke.

She steeled herself to receive his wrath when the sheriff rescued her. "Pastor Darl, you'll forgive me for agreeing with Agent…"

"Last."

"Agent Last." Sheriff Lowell sighed, placing a hand on the pastor's elbow once more. "The logic of her argument is sound. And you do want us to find the killer."

"And it's important that we interview every known person to a victim for several other reasons." Emma held up a finger. "One, it's important that we gather as much valuable evidence as possible for reasons that should be self-explanatory."

"And two?" the pastor asked through gritted teeth.

Emma added a second finger to the first. "If we don't, a good defense attorney can state that we targeted their client too quickly without considering every potential suspect. That can create reasonable doubt for a jury. I'm sure, once we catch the person who committed these horrible crimes, you won't want them freed because we didn't do our job properly." Emma cocked her head. "Would you?"

The pastor gripped his Bible as if the book were a balloon that could carry him out of this situation. After a few seconds passed, he nodded in silent agreement.

Jacinda gestured for Emma to take her seat again. The SSA stepped toward the sheriff and pastor, addressing them more formally. She had a knack for reading the room. "We appreciate all cooperation, Pastor Darl. To that end, I'd like to request a complete list of Little Clementine's citizens. Can you also make notation on who does and does not attend services here at Jubilant Ridge?"

The church leader laughed bitterly. "Such notations won't be necessary, I assure you. There isn't a soul in Little Clementine who isn't faithful to my house of God."

The sheriff sighed—a little too obviously, to Emma's way of thinking—and the pastor went redder around the collar. No love was lost between these two, despite the sheriff's attempts at cooperation.

"Pastor Darl, this team is here to do a job. Please let them."

Pastor Darl's mouth fell open. "This team is here to deliver the Lord's justice, with respect to His house of faith! They are here working in my church and among my flock, Sheriff!"

Emma tightened her lips into a flat line, staring forward. Beside her, Leo shifted in his seat.

She wasn't worried about the pastor erupting into outright violence—he struck her as too formal, too rigid—but she wasn't there to find the "Lord's justice."

At the edge of the group, Jacinda examined the evidence photos.

Emma respected her supervisor's focus but doubted how much headway they could make in this church basement. She followed Jacinda's gaze. The photos themselves seemed soaked in blood, not just the victims in them.

What the hell did she get us into here?

8

Pastor Darl scribbled out names on a sheet of paper, assuring the sheriff that he could list each member of his congregation alphabetically and by memory. Mia lingered off to the side, mostly observing Pastor Darl, while her colleagues congregated around the crime board.

By standing in on their briefing like some sort of entitled, grandiose avatar for the Lord, then doing a one-eighty and deciding to help—hoping to appear benevolent and important—the pastor might as well have had the word *Narcissist* tattooed across his forehead in Mia's humble—

That doesn't mean he'd axed people into their graves, but even so, signs are signs.

If this was the shepherd, Mia was concerned about the flock.

Pastor Darl's first red flag was a lack of empathy for the victims.

Ever since Mia and her team had stepped foot on his church's "hallowed ground," the good pastor had been all about the good pastor. He understood his congregation better than anyone else. The situation was all about him. His outbursts and arguments had little to do with the lost members of his so-called flock.

There was no doubt in Mia's mind that none of the blame would fall on his shoulders, even if he turned out to be the perpetrator. She imagined he would say the Devil worked in mysterious ways. He was a man of God.

No culpability. Another sign.

His second red flag—displaying impulsivity in his offer of a full list of names. Then showing a laughable amount of arrogance by providing names and addresses without assistance.

Mia felt sure, if she pressed the sheriff, she'd discover Pastor Darl had insisted local law enforcement use this basement as a base of operations. That way, he could insert himself and his opinion into the whole investigation.

She straightened and turned away from the superficially helpful pastor as Jacinda and Vance approached her.

Remember, this pastor's faulty moral compass doesn't make him a killer. Even arrogant, self-centered assholes can go their whole lives without murdering a single soul...physically, at least.

"Observing our good pastor?" Vance's whisper didn't carry beyond their small circle, but the intimacy of the gesture brought a slight blush to Mia's cheeks. The man really was too smooth for his own good.

"Can't hurt, right?" Mia shrugged, turning her gaze to Jacinda. "I'm ready to get to work, though. We about to split up and get a move on?"

"We're not going far yet. A lot of the people we need to talk to are upstairs." Vance pointed to the ceiling. "Jacinda's putting you and me on Bo Somerson."

Jacinda headed toward the basement door. "There's a small Sunday school room upstairs. Pastor Darl recommended we use it. We don't want to interview people down here anyway. People will take one look at that murder board and freak out."

The SSA set a fast pace, and Mia rushed up the stairs behind her. "A deputy just went to get Somerson and his family. Bo is Wade Somerson's son."

"Wade Somerson, the photographer who last saw our victims alive?"

"Yes. Since Wade is notably absent from the gathering outside, Bo's statements will be the next best thing until we track Wade down. His wife and stepdaughters are coming down with him to speed things along. Here you go."

The Sunday school room was painted an egg-yolk yellow. A portrait of Mary with Baby Jesus dominated one wall. Small tables and stubby-legged chairs littered the room. Boxes of used toys and shelves of worn books lined every corner. Children's handprints painted on construction paper decorated the walls with *Jesus loves me* emblazoned across each one.

Mia and Vance exchanged concerned looks. She knew he was thinking the same thing—how were they going to conduct a serious interview squatting on these tiny chairs? It had been a long time since Mia was a kindergartner.

As if hearing their concerns, Jacinda turned to them, looking grim. "Do your best." Without a backward glance, their supervisor headed back to the basement.

"She might set this whole place on fire before we're done in this town." Vance looked around the room again, as if he were contemplating where to help Jacinda spread fire accelerants. "There's no way anyone will take us seriously."

"We can make them take us seriously." Already, Mia was considering what little they knew of Wade Somerson. From the briefing, he was older and widowed and had been the last to see all their victims alive. His son should provide a more detailed background.

The man who appeared in the doorway beside the deputy wasn't much older than she was—maybe in his early thirties—and would have blended into any crowd.

An easy, wandering gaze and brown hair offset his baby face in a way that made him immediately nondescript. A petite blond woman followed him in. Two teenage girls, both in short skirts and tights under their winter coats, stood behind her. They couldn't have been more than sixteen years old, if that, and each boasted more makeup than Mia had ever worn in her life.

Small-town family. Teenagers rebelling and ready to escape. Nothing remarkable yet.

Mia shook Bo's hand, then Mrs. Somerson's. The teenagers each lifted a hand in a quick wave, which Mia returned. "I'm FBI Special Agent Mia Logan."

"And I'm Special Agent Vance Jessup." Vance offered Mrs. Somerson one of the grade school chairs, pulling it out for her before leaning against the wall himself.

To her credit, Mrs. Somerson settled herself with more grace than Mia could have managed. Bo sat beside his wife. The teenage girls remained standing, which was for the best, considering the length of their skirts, tights or no.

Mia took a seat across the small table from Bo, ignoring the girls' intense glances. Dying of curiosity, no doubt, or they'd have been off somewhere with their friends.

"Mr. Somerson—"

"I know why you're here." He clasped his hands and leaning forward. Bo Somerson's eyes bored into hers without blinking. "But you're up the wrong tree. I know Dad was the last one to see both the Murrays and the Crawfords. I understand him not being here now looks bad, but that ain't it. My father loves this town, this church, and its people. Every one of 'em. Everything about Little Clementine. He'd never do anything to hurt the flock, period."

Bo Somerson didn't see himself, his wife, his father, Wade, or anyone else in Little Clementine as "separate" people. They were all one and the same. The *flock* of this little church.

Mia sneaked a quick glance over at Vance, and he nodded just enough to show her they were on the same page. There were no individuals here in this town…just a congregation. A crowdsourced brain.

Mia smiled, hoping to pacify the man in front of her.

"I'm Lizbet." Mrs. Somerson leaned forward in her chair, resting her forearms on her knees. To Mia, she looked like a kindergarten teacher, getting down to Mia's level. Lizbet Somerson's focus flitted between Mia and Vance. "I'm Bo's wife. We just got married, and Wade's my father-in-law. Nicest man who ever lived. Did you know he's a widower? He's been alone for years. But he's still devoted to his wife after all this time. A man like that doesn't…doesn't kill."

Mia could show her dozens of headlines that countered that notion. Anyone could kill in the right—or wrong—circumstances.

The daughters, blond and green-eyed like their mother, crept closer to the table as Lizbet spoke. The shorter one tapped one perfect nail on the nearby wall as if for effect. "Grandpa's a good man. He wouldn't hurt nobody."

Vance crossed his arms. "It's not that we don't believe you, Miss Somerson—"

"Maybelle Sweeney, at your service." Maybelle adopted a pout that made her stepfather frown, but she nodded and walked around Mia and the table to face Vance head-on. She gave a little sniff as she approached, like she was picking up Vance's cologne. She took another bold step forward.

Vance didn't give ground, and his neutral face backed Maybelle up half a step.

The girl grinned, straightening her back and placing her hands on her narrow hips.

Vance raised an eyebrow but gave no other reaction to the girl's obvious attempt at flirting.

Mia tamped down a chuckle as Vance addressed the precocious child.

"Right, Maybelle, was it? We have to follow all leads, talk to everyone. And since your grandfather was so, ah, connected to the victims, we have to talk to him. You understand that, don't you?"

Mia bit her lip, unable to decide between watching the flirtatious spectacle or the scandalized expressions of the parents sitting nearby. She settled for a tennis-match-style back-and-forth.

"Grandpa Wade is a good, God-fearing man full of the Lord's light. He just wouldn't do a thing to hurt anyone!"

The other teenager inched around to stand by her sister so that they had poor Vance nearly cornered. But she didn't close the distance quite as much as her sister had. "Maybelle's right."

"Thanks for your input, Miss…"

"April Sweeney."

Lizbet spoke up again. "My girls are right. Bo and I only married two weeks ago, but Wade Somerson has accepted us all, as if we've been married the last twenty years. He's something special. Something good and righteous."

Vance stood straighter, ignoring the fawning looks the girls both gave him as he addressed their parents. "I'm assuming the girls' birth father is no longer present in the community. Is that correct?"

Bo Somerson stiffened in his chair. "That's right. Yes. I'm…I'm Lizbet's second husband. Her first, Archibald Sweeney, is with the Lord now."

Before either Mia or Vance could speak up, Lizbet

chimed in. "He died of a heart attack. It was so sudden. Just… one day he was there, and the next he wasn't. The girls were just seven and eight when it happened."

A soft rustle of fabric caught Mia's attention. Maybelle had dropped her coat to the ground and stood beside Vance. She was leaning sideways to give him more of a view down her low-cut blouse.

Had she undone some buttons while her mother was talking about the girls' father dying suddenly?

While Vance remained stoic against the boy-crazy teenager, Mia noted the parents flushed with embarrassment. Neither adult actually stepped in to correct their errant daughters' maneuvers, however.

Maybelle and April Sweeney practically crawled over Vance as he made a valiant attempt to fit in his questioning. The scene might have come out of an old comedy.

Had the girls ever seen a man outside of Little Clementine? They certainly didn't behave as if they had.

And while Mia couldn't blame the girls—Vance was quite handsome—this behavior was more than a little ridiculous.

Overtly promiscuous behavior at this age could indicate previous sexual abuse.

But she wasn't going to leap to any conclusions yet. Mia put the idea in the back of her mind and let it percolate.

In the meantime, watching Vance dodge their efforts was entertaining. He was such a gentleman that the girls couldn't have found a safer target.

Vance stepped sideways, causing April to stumble as she moved to press against his side. Mia turned back to Lizbet and Bo, instead of observing the painful awkwardness further.

Lizbet kept her head and body frozen in place, appearing to ignore her daughters' behavior. "Wade is such a talented photographer. He has an ability to capture the inner grace of whatever his subject is. He's been photographing the entire flock."

Across from her, Vance gained her admiration all over again as he steadfastly dodged every small assault the girls attempted.

Turning to Bo, Mia asked, "If your father isn't here with the flock, where exactly is he? And why wouldn't he be here if all you say is true?"

A few tears leaked from Lizbet's eyes. Mia passed her the small pocket pack of tissues she kept in her coat for just such occasions.

Bo licked his lips. "Right, uh, well, he must be at home. I'll give you his number and address."

"He's at home? We thought he was out of town."

"No, he's just not at the church. He was overcome with sorrow when he heard about the murders. Grief hits him hard, 'specially since we lost my mom. And we're all so close."

"Right." Mia sighed. "I know you are. But we need that address."

Lizbet balled up a second tissue and wrapped one arm around her husband's elbow, gripping him tight. Vance leaned in, shaking loose from the teenage terrors, and placed a pen and paper in front of Bo.

Bo squinted down at the paper, not yet writing. "It isn't right that a man is suspected of wrongs just because he don't have a wife to back up his innocence. Me, I'm always either working a carpentry job around other folks or with my family. My dad's been alone since my mom, Grace, died almost fifteen years ago. Dad hasn't been the same since. I doubt the man will ever remarry."

"Your father's marital status isn't the reason we need to speak with him." Vance squatted beside the Sunday school table.

Bo set the pen's nub to the paper, finally seeming about to

write, but stopped himself. He glanced between the two agents, Vance having temporarily disengaged from the teenagers pouting nearby. Bo finally settled on Mia, and he stared at her. "Does Dad being alone make him a monster capable of these sins? These murders? You can't believe that."

Mia shook her head but pointed to the paper in front of Somerson. "It doesn't, I promise you. But we still need to talk to him. We're not accusing him of anything. Just asking questions as part of the process. Since he was the last to see the victims, he may also have seen or heard something important. We won't be able to catch the perpetrator without him."

The man finally leaned over the table to write.

A little thump drew Mia's attention to Maybelle Somerson, who leaned her elbow theatrically against the wall. She was still trying to get Vance's attention.

Mia bit her lip, a laugh building. *That poor man.*

Across from her, Bo stopped writing and wrapped an arm around his wife. Mia reached forward to sweep up the paper, barely glancing down to verify that she could read the numbers and address.

Maybelle Sweeney had definitely undone a few more of those little pearl buttons. *It's time to get Vance out of this Sunday school before the girl tries to show him her damn birthday suit.*

If what Mia suspected turned out to be true, they'd need to look more closely at the Somerson household before they were through.

9

Leo led the way up the church basement's stairs, Agent Denae Monroe on his heels. The two were headed off to interview Ian Darl, the son of Pastor Gregory Darl. The pastor assured them Ian would be in the church office, just behind the pulpit, where he could always be found. Gregory informed them Ian was preparing to take over the congregation when the pastor retired.

Apparently, the father had warned the son they were on the way. A tall, fit man stood waving to them from the doorway, a friendly smile on his face. Leo and Denae started in his direction.

Denae spoke under her breath, low enough that only Leo heard her. "Doesn't look as off-putting as his father."

Leo smiled and spoke just as quietly, waving as they approached. "Let's hope so. But don't forget he's the heir apparent."

But even in the first few seconds, it was clear to Leo that Ian inherited his mannerisms from somewhere else. His mother, maybe. The man had an open honesty to his face that welcomed the agents. And he wore a neat button-down and khakis, which made Leo wonder if his mother still dressed him.

"Welcome to Little Clementine." Ian's smile broadened and ushered them into the office.

The space was exactly what Leo might've expected. One main desk, large and cluttered with paperwork. Side tables and repurposed nightstands spread around the edges of the room to hold hymnals, plants, more stacks of paper, and the requisite coffee maker. A few trays holding what looked to be homemade muffins, probably stale, completed the clutter.

For some reason, the idea of such sweetness turned Leo's stomach. He stole a quick glance out the grimy window to escape the claustrophobic space, however momentarily.

Instead, beyond the window, an army of thick trees closed in on the church.

No escape there.

Ian waved them into some chairs across from the desk. "Can I get you some coffee? Water? A muffin, perhaps? They're raspberry cinnamon, Mrs. Holmes's specialty."

Denae settled into one of the threadbare armchairs and crossed one leg over the other. A spring squeaked somewhere deep in the chair. "Just coffee would be great. Black, please."

"Ditto, if it's not too much trouble." Leo took a deep breath as he sat down. Unlike Denae's chair, his had no support. He sank so deep into the cushion, he wondered if his butt was on the ground. Leo uselessly shifted his weight, gave up, and slid out his iPad. He rested the device on his knees.

Ian prepared three cups and brought them over on a little silver tray that must've been in use for a century, if not longer.

Leo took a cup. "Ian, I understand you're the church organist?"

"And I give a sermon once in a while." His front two teeth were slightly crooked, which only made him seem more down-to-earth. "Look, before we go on, do you mind if I address one of the elephants in the room?"

Leo tried to maintain his balance between the coffee and his iPad. He probably looked like an idiot. But he kept his tone professional and authoritative. "Speak freely, please."

Any information they didn't have to steal and finagle from the pastor's fingers would be more than welcome.

"I want to apologize for my father's excitability. I assure you it's purely out of love for the people of this town and the deep concern he holds for their well-being." Ian sipped his coffee, gave a little sigh of contentment, and leaned back in his worn desk chair. "My father is, of course, very upset over the speculation about Wade Somerson potentially being involved with the murders. They've been best friends since… well, since before I was born."

I bet this town'll be a lot better off once this man takes over the pastorship. His dad probably takes his cues from Sinners in the Hands of an Angry God *more than the Good Book.*

Denae leaned forward, setting down her coffee on the edge of the desk. She could obviously get out of her seat. *Lucky her.* "Ian, we understand everyone in this town is very close. It's a matter of protocol—"

"To talk to everyone, I understand." Leo couldn't help thinking Ian seemed oddly at ease for someone who'd recently lost four close acquaintances, possibly friends. "But I just want to make sure you understand that I, myself, would be just as suspect as Wade if I hadn't chosen to sleep at my parents' house the last few nights. Normally, I'm home alone, just like Wade, as I've chosen to devote my life to God rather than marrying."

"Point taken." Leo pulled Ian's focus back. "But, with that said, could you tell us why you chose to sleep at home these last few nights? Was something keeping you on edge? Something odd you'd seen or heard in town, maybe?"

Ian squinted at him, as if confused, then gave another easy smile. "No, nothing like that."

His easy smile seemed like a habit. Seeing it this time, Leo wondered whether there was a speck of actual friendliness underneath the expression. "So…?"

"I'm moving. Most of my possessions are packed. Until my apartment lease is active in a week or so, I'm staying with them."

"May I ask why you're moving?" Denae's tone was light and encouraging. "We were under the impression you were training to be the next pastor. You give sermons regularly, right?"

Ian set his coffee down. "I didn't say 'regularly.' Once a month at most, and my father prefers it be just once per quarter, as the seasons change." For a moment, he stared out the window. Whether he was contemplating the rest of Denae's question or the nature of the nearby trees, Leo couldn't tell. Both agents let the silence linger. More often than not, silence was more effective than questioning to get someone to open up.

And finally, Ian did. "My dad is in denial. I'm not happy here. This community, while family, is too confining, too rigid."

"Rigid?" Denae took another sip of her coffee. Leo knew she was trying to keep it casual.

We're all just friends here, Ian. That was the message to send.

"Rigid. There are…rules. And there's little mercy for those who break them."

A small jolt of electricity burst under Leo's skin. Ian Darl wanted to talk, he could tell. In a few more minutes, they'd have a direction for their investigation.

"Did the Crawfords or the Murrays break the rules?"

"No. If anything, they set the rules. Pillars of the community."

Leo and Denae remained quiet, waiting for him to expand on "pillars of the community." The coffee cup felt burning hot against Leo's fingers.

Instead, Ian gave a mirthless chuckle. "Staying with my parents the last few nights, while a necessity, proved to be lucky in hindsight. God was on my side, it appears, guiding my actions, as He so often does. I hope He guides your actions as well?"

Leo ignored the question. "Do you know anyone in the community who may have had a vendetta against either the Murrays or the Crawfords?"

A sharp voice answered before Ian could. "A vendetta? We're not the Mafia, Agent Ambrose."

Pastor Gregory Darl stood in the office doorway. His body filled the space.

Leo tried to stand, but between the low seat, his coffee, and his iPad, he couldn't move gracefully.

Denae came to his rescue. She stood and squared off with the pastor. "Pastor Darl, you're interrupting an official interview. I'm going to have to ask you to leave."

"This is my church—"

"And this is my interview. If you're as interested in catching the perpetrator as we are, I assume you don't want to interfere with our process?"

The pastor's cheeks glowed red, but to Leo's surprise, the man nodded and stepped back. Gregory cast a sharp glance at his son. "Be cooperative, Ian."

"I am, Father."

Denae stepped up to the pastor. "Thank you, Pastor." She shut the door in his face.

Leo might've fallen in love with her a little just then.

She returned to her chair.

Denae reached for her coffee but changed her mind and sat back without it. Leo, once again, envied her range of motion. "How about angry, then? Anyone angry at either Mr. Murray or Mr. Crawford in particular?"

Ian shrugged, sipping the watery coffee. Then he shut down before Leo's eyes. His shoulders hunched. He held the coffee cup with both hands, his fingers curled around the porcelain like a talisman.

"Possibly. We're all sinners. But I'm not privy to the secrets of the Crawfords or Murrays."

Disappointment washed over Leo. The man had been ready to talk. After his father's interruption, it'd take a miracle to work the son's bravery back up.

Denae seemed to sense the change as well. She shifted them in a different direction, gesturing to some family photos hanging on the wall. "And do you or your father have access to any of the photos Wade Somerson took? Maybe of the church? I understand he's been working on a community directory."

"He's been working on a directory for the church, which is our community."

Ian's correction was gentle but pointed...the first sign of his father's influence coming through.

Damn Pastor Darl's interference.

"But to answer your question, no, I don't believe anyone besides Wade has access to those photos. So they'll be in his possession. I don't see what you'll gather from pictures of church folks smiling into a camera, but what do I know about investigations and the sort of work you do?"

Leo slid his iPad back into its coat. They needed to give Ian space to rebuild his courage. "We appreciate your time, Ian. I assume you'll be available if we have any further questions?"

"Of course." Ian leaned forward over the desk, not speaking until Leo met his gaze. "If you need any assistance in arranging interviews, I'm at your service. My father can be a real wolf when it comes to defending his parish."

Leo's gut clenched at the word *wolf*, and he couldn't help but suck in a quick breath. His usual smile slipped for a moment.

Across from him, Ian's eyes glinted in recognition. "Not a fan of wolves, Agent Ambrose?" Ian was a perceptive one, all right. "I don't blame you. As a shepherd, I've been taught it's my duty to protect my flock from wolves. I hope you're a better shepherd than me. Please protect us. I've clearly failed."

Forcing a nod, his smile back in place, Leo willed the picture of that nightmare wolf to fade into the background of his thoughts.

But, despite Ian Darl's easy smile and the quiet calm of the church office, he couldn't help feeling a threat in the air.

Not from Ian, but from someone. Somewhere.

The murderer in this town might be a proverbial wolf in sheep's clothing.

Dang it, it's just superstitions getting to me.

But right now, today, in this office, the superstitions felt real.

A sheen of sweat formed under his hairline. He needed to get out.

Leo stood, managing the maneuver from the sunken chair in one grand move. Aware of Denae's dark eyes on him, he nodded toward the door. "If you'll excuse me, I think I just need a breath of fresh air. Allergies must be getting to me."

The excuse was thin. Denae covered up his awkward exit by asking something about Ian's normal routine.

Thankful for her help, he hurried past the pulpit toward

the church's main entrance. At the last minute, he veered left toward a side door and stepped out onto a small porch.

As he'd hoped, Leo managed to avoid most of the townspeople crowded around the front of the building. In the distance, their voices mingled, wondering out loud over what evil had befallen their small town. That word, *evil*, rang out over others, a symptom of how religious the whole town was.

He muttered under his breath, breathing in and out fast. "The sooner we get this damn case solved, the better."

The fresh air wasn't helping. Beyond the gravel lot surrounding the church, he saw only woods and mountains. The woods were too thick, the mountains too tall, and the whole scene left him feeling trapped. He clenched the handrail of the little side porch. The Jubilant Ridge House of Faith loomed at his back.

In his nightmare, he'd gripped his grandparents' porch rail exactly as he held the handrail now.

Leo stumbled away to the side of the church, leaning down and focusing his breath as he gripped his knees, shaking off the similarity of position.

He forced himself to stand straight.

Instead of focusing on the mountains ahead, beyond the woods, he stared at the Bureau's SUVs parked in the lot just in front of him.

Any one of them capable of allowing a hiding place, a shelter, an escape—if or when that was needed.

He barked out a quiet laugh, stifling the sound with his fist.

"Since when am I claustrophobic? What the hell?"

His chest ached. He couldn't bear to look at the surrounding woods and mountains. They felt like insurmountable prison walls. His breath was coming a touch too fast. He imagined his smile, frozen on his face, appeared more like a Halloween mask than anything else.

The image of the beheaded Rosemary Crawford came to him suddenly, overlaying the SUVs like a curtain as he remembered his dream wolf's words.

"The path to the wolf is covered in innocent blood."

"Whose blood?" The whisper leaked from his lips. His question seemed to linger like smoke on the breeze.

He wasn't even close to finding an answer.

10

Pastor Gregory Darl led Emma and Jacinda upstairs to the second floor of the church, then through a maze of rooms that once served as a home for the Darl family.

Julianna Darl, Pastor Darl's wife and Ian's mother, trailed behind meekly. She stood a bit taller than Emma but seemed far more diminutive. Her mouse-brown hair was braided back. Passive brown eyes studied the upper level with a strange, surreal calm.

Emma couldn't get a read on the woman.

Julianna Darl could've been a benevolent mother figure to the community or a bitter, silent woman who resented everyone around her. In their short acquaintance, either possibility had equal odds of being true in Emma's estimation.

The upper floor offered space that was, as the good pastor put it, used as needed. Cots, boxes of supplies, and blankets littered every room.

Eventually, Emma and Jacinda found themselves following the pastor and his wife into a nursery. When Julianna Darl flicked on the overhead light, Emma paused.

Antique cribs littered the corners of the room. A little circle of rocking chairs stood stiffly in the center of the space. Fading floral wallpaper shrank the already-tiny space, making it seem like an overdecorated dollhouse. And there were bars on all the windows, turning the place into a miniature jailhouse of sorts, rendering it ripe for a bloody ghost baby to appear.

Emma faltered just inside the doorway.

Please, please, please, don't give me any ghost babies.

And the thought of ghost babies speaking to her when real babies couldn't use words made Emma shiver as she eyed every crib in the room.

All the cribs remained empty. No ghosts to be seen. Infant or otherwise.

For once, the universe listened to her pleas, and the chill she'd felt was all in her head.

Julianna motioned Emma forward.

Jacinda had already taken a seat across from the pastor in one of the rocking chairs. The SSA tilted the chair back and forth, cutting through the dust and cobwebs of Emma's imagination—the wooden chairs had been well kept.

Both Pastor Darl and Jacinda looked at her oddly. But Julianna Darl held a plastic, pleasant smile in place, the picture of a quintessential pastor's wife.

Emma moved into the room, willing her steps to remain even and calm.

Pastor Darl gestured at the space with a nod, as if pleased with himself. "These upstairs rooms are mostly used when the power goes out or a member of our congregation is in need of temporary housing. Trees fall through roofs in winter storms. Electricity goes out and a baby needs warmth. Last year, a bear broke into the Osborne house and set up shop in the kitchen. You can't expect a family to live through that."

His wife *tsked*. "It was such a mess. And them with three little children to care for. We put them up here until the bear was caught and their kitchen was back in order."

The pastor nodded. "The Christian thing to do. Are you Christians, Agents?"

Jacinda coughed, letting her rocking chair go still, and Emma decided to let her handle this one. She was the boss, right? Besides, Emma was having a difficult time keeping her eyes off the damn cribs.

"If you don't mind, Pastor, our faith," she gestured to herself and her team, "is not a matter for discussion here." Jacinda opened her iPad, doing an admirable job of remaining still and steady in her rocking chair.

Emma would have laughed if she wasn't practically frozen for fear a spirit would jump out at her.

The pastor and his wife kept the same Oscar-winning smiles on their faces, until he unclenched his jaw to speak.

"Of course, of course, my apologies. Still, this is a God-fearing town." His blue eyes darted between Emma and Jacinda. Judging them. "You'll do well to remember that. My people will respect you more for it. I daresay God's hands will be guiding you in your investigation all the more if you welcome Him into your hearts."

I bet I know a bit more about how the afterlife will help this investigation than you, Pastor.

Pleasant but blank smile still in place, Julianna stood just behind her husband's rocking chair.

Stepford wife much?

"Yes, well, be that as it may…" Jacinda glanced at Emma, one eyebrow raising just fast enough for Emma to catch it. It was good to know her supervisor questioned this guy's attitude too. "What can you tell us about the victims? Any disagreements they might've had with any of your other parishioners?" Jacinda offered a phony smile of her own, looking a bit like a toothpaste commercial. "Surely, everyone came to you with their problems?"

Pastor Darl preened for a moment. He rocked back and forth in his chair, its struts creaking as he did. Then he shrugged off Jacinda's question.

"Oh no, you misunderstand our community. There are no disagreements here…none of consequence, at least…and we take care of our own. Some interloper from out of the mountains is our murderer, I promise you."

Emma leaned in a bit toward Julianna Darl. "Mrs. Darl, perhaps Rosemary Crawford or Louise Murray confided in you about some troubles, woman to woman?"

Rather than answering, the woman pursed her lips and shook her head, looking at her husband for guidance.

Gregory Darl brought his wife's hand to his shoulder. Emma noted Julianna's fingers remained on him, even after he released her.

The pastor offered a smile that didn't quite reach his eyes. "If they had, I assure you, my wife would've confided those troubles to me. We seek guidance from the Lord together. Female confidences and gossip hold no weight in the eyes of the Lord our Father, who sees all."

The pastor's smile was maddening. Emma saw no charisma in it, so she glanced back to his nodding wife. "Julianna, I'd love to hear from you—"

"My wife is a woman of faith." Pastor Darl's volume was coming close to a shout. "She would've spoken up already if she had any pertinent information to share."

Emma stood straighter, frowning down at the pastor.

And I'd like to feed you to a ghost and see if you had any pertinent information for me then, you old goat.

Jacinda's white-knuckle grip on the chair's arms mirrored Emma's frustration. She started rocking double time, her annoyance broadcast by each creak of the chair, even as she attempted to appear casual.

"Pastor Darl, we do need to hear from both you and your wife. Now, if you'd be so kind as to tell us about the victims' relations with other parishioners, we'd very much appreciate it."

As the pastor continued in his *my flock loves each other without fail* mode, Emma observed Julianna Darl nodding at his every word like a damn puppet. Julianna's hand remained on the man's shoulder, too, even though it must've been awkward to keep pace with his rocking. He seemed to have forgotten Julianna was present. The woman remained maddeningly silent.

Had her husband told her to avoid their questions and let him talk?

Emma steeled herself to speak over the pastor and address Julianna once more.

Footsteps thundered up the stairs. Both rocking chairs froze.

Jacinda rose and stepped to one side, setting her iPad on the chair seat. Emma pivoted and moved the other direction. Both agents' hands hovered near their firearms as they focused on the door.

An elderly man with wide blue eyes and sparse white hair stopped in a huff, blockading the nursery's doorway. "What right do you government busybodies have taking up so much of my son's righteous minutes on this earth?"

Emma was tired of these people. "We—"

"Your presence is almost enough cause to take the Lord's great name in vain!"

She dropped her hand from her holster.

Jacinda sighed and moved closer to Emma.

The pastor stood to place himself between them and the intruder.

"This is my father, retired pastor of our great church, Bud Darl. I apologize for the intrusion, but—"

"Don't you apologize for me!" The old man stomped inside, planting himself directly in front of Emma and Jacinda.

Emma nudged the nearest rocking chair backward with her foot, sensing Jacinda doing the same. They might need room to maneuver in the space at this rate.

"Sir," Jacinda held one hand up between them, "if you'll take a step back and—"

"Why are you here?" Spittle flew from the man's lips.

Emma was vaguely aware of Julianna taking a tissue from her skirt and wiping her face. It would've been comical if it hadn't been Julianna's life. A spurt of pity shot through her.

"Sir, we—"

"You should be out looking for the psychotic devil-snake outsider who shed blood in our God-fearing town and interrupted our peace. Not interrogating God's kingdom. How dare you! How dare the government!"

The man stepped closer, coming within a foot of Jacinda, who gave no ground. "Sir," she tried again. "We—"

"Father." Gregory Darl tugged at his dad's arm, his composure slipping for the first time.

Sweat ran from Pastor Darl's forehead. The grin on his face was more a skull's rictus than any expression of cheer as Bud's coat sleeve puckered beneath his son's tight fingers.

Bud shook his son off and held up a straight arm, silencing him.

Julianna stood frozen at the side of the nursery, calling no attention to herself, so Emma kept her eyes on Bud Darl.

"You want to interrogate me now? Another man of God?" He stepped forward, coming within a foot of Jacinda and sneering. "I'm an old man with no alibi, either, just like Wade Somerson. I was sleeping in my trailer behind Gregory's house during all the murders. Alone. Maybe." The man paused and emitted a high-pitched cackle.

His son threw up his hands as if in despair, or maybe in a last-ditch prayer. "Dad, please don't—"

"You fancy federal agents gonna arrest me for not having anyone watch me sleep when those fine folks were killed?" The old man all but growled, his fists clenched. "That your plan?"

Julianna flinched backward against one of the cribs.

Inching her hand back toward her handcuffs, Emma prepared to arrest the old man, just like he'd suggested.

The man was a bully, presenting himself as an absolute monster. Emma would gladly make him reap what he'd sown. Man of God or not.

Jacinda, however, proposed a judicious retreat. "We'll be talking with you, Mr. Darl, but we can certainly give you time to settle down."

"I am perfectly calm! I—"

"I'd think twice before raising your voice to a federal agent." The steel in Jacinda's tone stopped Bud short. "Agent Last and I are going to step out now. But we'll be in touch soon, Mr. Darl. Pastor Darl. Mrs. Darl. Please feel free to pray about your situation."

11

Driving to Wade Somerson's residence was a relief for Leo. He felt as if he'd escaped an afternoon in prison. From the beginning, this case had set his teeth on edge.

Give my nerves some time to reset before I'm back at the church.

Or in Emma's passenger seat.

Beside him, Denae pointed to a run-down Victorian at the side of the road. "That's gotta be it. Nothing else in sight. We're about out of road."

Three stories tall, the old home must've been beautiful once. It was now badly in need of an updated paint job and new porch steps. With its peeling paint and missing shutters, the structure appeared to be one bad storm away from being declared condemned.

An old pickup squatted in the driveway, suggesting Wade was home.

Leo parked by the curb and played hopscotch across a series of cracked pavers to avoid a mostly mud yard. Denae went the long way around, pacing him down the cracked driveway.

He knocked on the doorframe. The screen on the storm door hung loose from one corner. "He's not advertising his maintenance skills, is he?"

The door creaked open, emitting a blast of warm air from the overheated house. "Who're you?"

"Mr. Somerson, I'm Special Agent Leo Ambrose, and this is Special Agent Denae Monroe."

A man with neat salt-and-pepper hair and dark eyes squinted out, then waved them inside. "Wondered what was takin' you so long. Come on in."

Leo followed Denae into what he immediately perceived as the antithesis of the home's exterior. Warm and cozy, with shiny hardwood flooring and soft lighting, the entryway opened into a living room with overstuffed furniture and a brightly burning fire.

Unlike everywhere else they'd visited in town, Leo felt more relaxed here. In the living room, he lowered himself into a seat across from Wade. "Mr. Somerson, we appreciate your time. We're here to—"

"I know why you're here." The man waved off the introductions, though not impolitely. More as if he simply had no use for small talk, which Leo could respect. "I was the last to see those poor folks alive before they were slaughtered. No other word for it. And I ain't got an alibi for my whereabouts on either of the evenings."

Wade straightened his cardigan. This man was willowy, almost as if he'd purposefully let himself age beyond his fifty-some years. Leo could see him choosing to sit by a crackling fire and while away a January afternoon with some whittling or a book of crosswords. It was difficult, if not impossible, to imagine him wielding an axe in the dead of night.

Denae leaned forward, her voice quieter than usual. "You were one of the few townsfolk not at the church today, Mr. Somerson."

"That's right. Didn't see any use in adding to the spectacle. If all that's enough to arrest me, y'all can go ahead and arrest me right now. But I didn't kill anybody. And I won't let y'all off the hook of investigating by telling you I did."

Papu would've liked this guy.

Leo sat back in his chair. "We're not here to arrest anyone. What you've told us might, at best, be enough for a search warrant, but we're not at that stage yet. We're just here to ask you some questions."

The man pursed his lips, narrowing his eyes, as if in frustration. "You don't need no warrant as far as I'm concerned, and I'm the only one on my deed. Search away."

Sharing a glance with Denae, Leo offered her a small shrug. "Invitation notwithstanding, we'll start with the questions. But I appreciate your willingness to help."

Denae pushed some of her curls back out of her face. "Mr. Somerson, can you tell us if you noticed anything off about the Crawfords when you photographed them?"

"I didn't." The man gazed into the fire. "My Grace might have, if she'd been here…she was always noticing everything, that woman…but I ain't big on getting into people's personal business. They seemed fine to me. Happy enough. But they wouldn't've talked to me in any case. Folks around here take their problems to two places and two places only…Pastor Darl and the Lord."

Sounds about like what we heard at the church. Figures.

Leo unzipped his coat and loosened his shirt collar. The fire's heat was just shy of causing him to sweat. With the dirty windows and otherwise dim light, he would've guessed they'd reached nighttime if he hadn't known better.

"But you'd have known if the couples were having trouble?" Denae asked. "Photographers notice details, right?"

Wade shook his head, frowning. "I shouldn't know what happens behind closed doors."

"How long had you known them?"

"Forever. Like everyone else in this town."

Leo opened his iPad, hoping the thing wouldn't melt in the heat. "And can you tell us what kind of men Mr. Crawford and Mr. Murray were? Maybe you recall some feuds they may have had with other locals, or even someone outside the area?"

"Chet was closest to my age. Ernie was about a couple years behind him. Both of 'em took care of their wives, took care of their homes, came to church, and loved their neighbors. Close to the pastors, both past and present."

"Good Christian folks." Denae's comment didn't come across with her usual sarcasm, but Leo caught the echo of all they'd been told at the church. "There must be something more, though?"

Wade pushed himself up with his hands on his knees and walked over to the varnished mantel above the fire. There, he picked up a photograph of a couple and stared at it before bringing the memento back to the seating area.

He held the framed picture up for the agents, making sure they both got a good look. The photo was of Somerson at a younger age, alongside a woman with lovely brown hair and brown eyes, her face open and bright.

"This is a picture of me and my Grace. Taken before she got sick. Would've been about fifteen years ago. Doctor gave her three to six months. She was gone in two. We were high school sweethearts."

"I'm sorry for your loss." And Leo was too. The grief in the old man's voice, shaking just a tiny bit, couldn't be faked. The emotion underlying his words reminded Leo of how Yaya spoke of her lost husband whenever his name came up.

"Thank you. The point is, this is the type of relationship this town is built on. Love. Loyalty. Forgiveness of one another when it's needed. Prayer. We're a small town with big worries, but we make do. We always have. What evil has come in and killed those four good men and women this past week…it won't stand. That's all I can tell you. There ain't no feuds here. Just good, God-fearing men and women who do their best for themselves and each other and follow the Good Book as best they can."

A few seconds of silence passed while Wade held the photo in his hands, as if the picture whispered secrets to him.

Denae caught Leo's eye and pointed toward the staircase, shrugging. Asking if they might as well search, given the old man's invitation.

They weren't getting anything incriminating from Wade's straightforward answers, so Leo supposed poking around made sense. "Sir, while we're here, we'll take you up on your offer to search your property. You have my word we won't damage anything."

The man barely reacted to Leo's words, more focused on his dead wife. "You two do what you need to. I'll be here. I'm always here."

His words held an odd ring—more doom than promise.

Leo didn't let himself dwell on the man's grief. Everyone had sorrows to carry. Dissecting them wouldn't make the emotion go away.

Instead, he moved with Denae farther into the well-kept house and began looking for whatever there was to find.

The kitchen was the only other room on the main floor. It offered no surprises whatsoever.

Upstairs, they found three bedrooms, one of which had blackout curtains and was set up as a makeshift photography studio. Candid shots and family portraits were scattered over every surface.

To one side, an old-school Polaroid camera sat atop a clipboard full of names, most of which had been checked off.

The other two bedrooms were neatly made up, one lived

in and one not. Leo guessed the empty one was Bo Somerson's old room.

No surprises.

Denae peered out the main bedroom's window. "Garage outside."

"Lead the way." Leo jiggled one last bureau drawer open, where he found a dusty photo of two teen boys. One looked like Ian Darl, skinnier and more awkward than his adult self, and the other Leo guessed was Bo Somerson. Both boys were in basketball uniforms and wore goofy smiles. "Looks like Bo didn't grab everything when he moved out." Leo finished replacing one of the bureau drawers, squeaking the furniture back together as he did.

Going down the stairs, Leo lingered on the photographs lining the wall. Most featured Wade Somerson and his wife, their arms around their son, Bo. Other images showed Bo at various moments of note, from football and basketball games to school dances and days spent fishing. Photos everywhere, all pointing to a happy family.

What had once been a happy family, at least.

The icy cold stripped away the residual heat of the house from every room but the one Wade had the fire going in. Leo zipped his coat again.

Outside the detached garage, the frame of a rusted pickup truck sat on cement blocks, and although the vehicle guarded the entrance of the structure, there wasn't much to be guarded.

Inside, they found a wide assortment of tools, mostly meant for plumbing.

"No axe." Denae crouched to peer beneath a workbench, shifting aside some unopened paint cans to see underneath. "And no bloody clothes. No signs of any trouble here or in the house."

"Not exactly a center of mayhem." Leo closed a toolbox and straightened. "Just…sadness."

"That's a bit poetic."

He shrugged. There was nothing to be found hidden in or around Wade's property.

Little Clementine was wearing on him.

"We had to check." Denae pulled the garage door shut behind them. "And at least this is one place down."

Leo peered into the rusted-out pickup trucks, one sitting abandoned in front of the garage and the slightly more usable one in the driveway—but only clean, if worn, bench seats greeted him.

Back in the Expedition, Leo sat behind the wheel again.

"What would make someone lose it and pick up an axe?" Denae postulated, pulling out her iPad to begin brainstorming based on what little they knew. "Taking an axe to two couples takes dedication, right? And rage…but no one's admitting to anger."

"Anger is a sin, and we're outsiders. They won't confess to us."

12

I cut my perfectly seasoned pork chop into smaller bites, then pushed them around the plate, giving the illusion I'd eaten more. Running the pork through the creamed corn and soaking up some of that butter would add flavor, but throwing away the remains of my food was just as tempting. Much as this meal would've made me salivate on some other day, I wasn't hungry.

My meal was a lonely one tonight. Everyone else stayed at the church, gossiping and arguing and worrying. Perhaps it was my duty to stay there as well, but I'd needed a break. I begged off with a headache.

I'd failed to consider how empty this place would be when alone.

As empty as my future.

Maybe if I prayed again…

"Oh, Lord, thank You for this harvest, for our daily bread and sustenance. For the seeds in the earth. Help me to remember Your provision and Your generosity as well as Your sacrifice. To be thankful for meals such as this bounty. In Your blessed name, I pray. Amen."

I opened my eyes, picked up my knife and fork once more, and stared at the meal in front of me.

Still, I barely saw it.

Hunger was nothing in the face of the evil set against me.

There was nothing appetizing about six federal agents setting up shop at our church.

I knew law enforcement would come in and get involved. Sooner rather than later.

But the Feds? FBI, no less?

I hadn't counted on that.

Forcing myself to take a bite of my pork chop, I washed the food down with a large gulp of water. The food wasn't dry, just my throat.

Sheriff Lowell was someone I could've dealt with just fine. Larry Lowell couldn't tell his face from his foot most of the time. The man didn't much care what happened to the citizens of Little Clementine. We were a backwoods town of zealots, so far as Lowell was concerned. He'd certainly ignored us long enough already. Every complaint discounted. Every woman hysterical. Every man reasonable.

In Lowell's hands, the case would've gone cold eventually. Written off as the work of some crazy person just passing through the county. A hitchhiker, most likely.

Outsiders were Sheriff Larry Lowell's excuse for most bad work in his jurisdiction.

"I have so much more to do. I'm not done yet." The whisper sat in the air, heavy as the meal on my plate.

I dropped my fork, letting the utensil clatter to the floor as I closed my eyes to shut out the secrets as well as the memories intruding on the dinner hour.

"You unholy bastard!"

The words stabbed at my brain again, like they did more and more often lately.

"You unholy bastard!"

No, I couldn't be done yet. Evil was still very much alive in my community, and I now had the task of vanquishing it while the FBI poked into every crook and cranny. There was no telling what they'd find out.

A scream built in my chest—the pressure as real as heartburn. I picked up my knife and stabbed the pork chop until pieces flicked from the plate, landing on the table and floor as greasy and peppered as the evil I struggled against.

When my limbs went loose and the urge to scream died, I bent from my chair and began cleaning up. I was better than this. Better than anyone knew.

The Lord worked in mysterious ways. He would clear the way for my work.

Maybe the average person would consider what I was doing to be murder.

Thankfully, I was far wiser than the average person.

13

Little Clementine's Heights of Glory Inn was falling apart. Complete with peeling wallpaper, water-stained ceilings, and rabbit-eared television sets, the place had last seen its prime some decades, possibly even centuries, earlier.

Emma switched to her left side and bunched the pillow tighter under her head. Beneath her, the ancient, lumpy mattress had no give. She imagined this mattress had caused many sleepless nights…back when the Puritans first used it.

Unfortunately, the firetrap of a resting place was the only lodging in Little Clementine, putting them within a short walk of their current home base.

Never thought I'd wish for a Harris Hotel, but here we are. I'll be lucky if I get an hour's rest tonight.

Emma stuffed a spare pillow under her head and rolled back to her right side. She shivered, pulling the threadbare quilt higher.

The extra cushioning was more like a feather-stuffed brick. Unable to find a position that didn't put her neck into a weird twist, she flung the added pillow away in frustration…directly toward the flash of a child ghost appearing in the corner.

Emma nearly jumped to the ceiling. "Sorry." Her voice was shakier than she liked. "I didn't see you."

The boy's white-eyed stare and pale face were already gone.

This had been the fourth ghost to appear in her room so far, and each one had turned the room into a freezer. The first had risen beside her bed to loom over her. While the ghost had a childlike stature and form, its presence exuded menace and gloom more so than even the ghost of a clown Emma had seen at the Ruby Red Spectacle Circus. And that ghost had a hole blown through its chest, with innards and blood leaking out.

At least the specters she'd encountered in Little Clementine had shown no signs of violent ends. So far.

Small mercies, Emma girl. Small mercies.

None of them had spoken. Not one word of explanation for their presence or how they might help Emma's team solve the murders. That, at least, was par for the course and gave her a small sense of comfort.

On the circus case, a dead trapeze artist had finally spoken, at the eleventh hour, and helped Emma apprehend the circus killer. Leaving her forced to invent explanations for Leo, who praised her inventiveness in talking the killer down and distracting him from taking another life.

How could she ever explain to her fellow agent that she'd only known what to say because a dead woman gave her the words?

Emma wasn't sure what she'd do the first time a ghost attempted to assist in a case right from the start.

Another child appeared in her room, at the foot of the bed this time. Its little head remained bowed as if in prayer, so she couldn't see the face or determine whether it was male or female. Like the others, this one stood still, didn't speak, and eventually dissipated into the cold air.

None of them gave her the slightest welcome, much like the rest of Little Clementine.

Maybe she should be thankful none of the ratty motel's ghosts wished to have a word with her, but for whatever reason, she wasn't.

Rolling onto her back, Emma stared at the water stain above the bed.

It's the frustration from the whole day that's getting to me. Not just the damn ghosts.

Above her, the bubbled ceiling tile mocked her, threatening to burst.

Her mind went back to the case and the frustration still gurgling in her gut from their end-of-day briefing at the church.

Pastor Darl had interrupted them twice, coming down from his office for no apparent reason but to butt in...even after promising to give them privacy. Both times, he'd burst in on conversations to emphasize how wrong the FBI's team had to be. His flock was "salt of the earth men and women who'd not hurt a fly, let alone each other."

Yet for all the dramatic speeches over the course of the day, information remained scarce. No one in town seemed to believe anyone else capable of murder...even though someone had clearly committed them.

Our axe murderer isn't a flickery ghost in need of anger management. It's someone in this town.

"Someone who knew them killed them."

The men had been focal points of incredible rage. To Emma's thinking, that level of rage only happened toward someone the murderer knew. Someone who'd betrayed them in some way. Someone who'd violated some kind of trust. This wasn't stranger danger.

By comparison, the women were killed cleanly, even with the multiple strikes made to Rosemary Crawford.

More than likely, the murderer was someone the victims had called a friend—possibly right up until the moment they'd died.

A member of their own so-called flock.

Yet without worthwhile information coming from the interviews, where did that kind of knowledge leave her team? Everyone in town knew everyone else and had relationships with each other. No useful evidence had been recovered from the crime scenes yet. The M.E.'s final tests could take weeks—whatever good more tests might do them.

Emma's breath puffed above her, and she almost brought the lumpy pillow over her face. But she'd probably suffocate.

Ghost number five? Six? How many have there been now?

She looked around.

The face of a ghastly thin little boy appeared beside her bed. Close enough to smack foreheads with Emma. She almost screamed in surprise but caught herself, immediately evaluating the kid.

No visible wounds, just like the others. That meant he'd probably died of illness.

The boy's furrowed brow and wrinkled nose were enough to communicate his distaste for her presence, but he said nothing.

Emma considered telling him to knock before entering a woman's room until the moment he vanished. The temperature in the room immediately rose.

"That's fine." She rolled over, shutting her eyes tight in annoyance. "I didn't want to talk to you anyway."

Though I kind of did.

A soft tap broke the silence. Emma groaned. She turned on the light on the nightstand. She'd had to request a new bulb from the front desk, and she'd received a nearly burned-out bulb that cast everything in an acidic glow. But she was grateful for it.

The tap sounded again. Emma picked up her gun and crept toward the door, her sock-clad feet not making a sound.

Creeping closer, Emma kept quiet and evened her breathing against her nerves. Approaching from the side, Emma pulled the curtain just askew enough that she could see outside.

Mia.

Releasing a sigh of relief, Emma dislodged the door chain and opened it. Like her, Mia wore sweats, though the other agent also had on sneakers and a coat.

Mia grinned, lifting what had to be a container filled with cookies. "I couldn't sleep. Thought you might be in the same boat. Care for a nighttime snack?"

Emma's mouth watered. "You have no idea. You're a lifesaver. Where'd you get them?"

"I made them a couple days ago and threw them in my go bag on the way out the door."

Whereas Emma couldn't have baked a cookie to save her life, Mia was practically a master baker when it came to sweets and breads.

"Ha. Well, I didn't want to eat them all alone anyway."

Mia followed Emma over to the bed. The two of them leaned back against the headboard in the dim light, the container of cookies open between them. Emma bit down on her first cookie. Chocolate chip with M&M's, just firm enough to offer a satisfying crunch. She *mmm*'d in satisfaction. "Seriously, these are fantastic."

The other agent grinned, breaking one apart and sliding a morsel peppered with red M&M's into her mouth. When she'd finished chewing, she pulled apart the rest of the cookie. "This town is something else, isn't it? I've never seen so many people who clearly have secrets bending over backward to convince us they're one big, happy family."

Emma snagged a bottle of water from the nightstand and took a long sip before passing the drink to her friend. "Darl's flock. They're certainly a tight-knit bunch. Any red flags for you yet?"

"Aside from the words coming out of every interviewee's mouth?" Mia laughed. "Not really. You heard what Vance said at the briefing. We got nothing."

Emma grinned. "Other than a bunch of hormones."

"Yeah, there is that. You should've seen those teenagers going all googly-eyed over Vance."

"Well, no more googly-eyed than a certain agent I know." Emma teased her friend with a nudge of her shoulder and grabbed another cookie.

"Uh-uh, you better lock me in a jail cell until I get my head on straight if I ever fawn over anyone like those girls did. Though, I wonder if their behavior indicates they've been hurt. Their parents didn't do anything, and they were throwing themselves at a grown man."

Emma nibbled at her cookie. "Could be. There are some strange things in this town." She ignored the ghost boy flitting in and out of the corner.

Then Mia cracked a small smile, revealing her dimples. "You should've seen Vance's face though." She gave Emma an impression of his bug-eyed expression, and Emma laughed.

Despite the ghosts in her room, and the axe murderer out there in the night, this was just what she'd needed.

14

Leo didn't actually flinch at the weak coffee being served in the church basement, but he did decide against sitting next to the scowling Denae Monroe. There'd be no living with her until they got her a stronger brew.

Perhaps predictably, the Heights of Glory Inn received so little business that they didn't bother serving anything to eat, not even a continental spread of day-old doughnuts and stale coffee. As a result, he and the rest of the team had experienced a rush of gratitude when they'd entered their church home base that morning and found hot coffee and homemade muffins provided by the Darls.

He wondered if this was how they inspired their flock. Knowing very little food was available on offer in town, the Darls provided average refreshments and gained everyone's favor. Leo liked them the tiniest bit better for feeding him. He was sure the pastor would open his mouth soon, though.

The weak coffee was something he'd live with. Denae, on the other hand…

Jacinda waved her half-eaten muffin at the coffee-obsessed agent, silencing a new complaint.

As Mia and Vance sat down, Jacinda began the briefing.

"As you all saw, the parking lot outside is full of Little Clementine's citizens...again...and protests are mounting over not being able to attend meetings held in their own church."

Vance laughed outright, covering his full mouth with one fist. "You mean *our* meetings? They want to attend FBI briefings?"

Beside Jacinda, Sheriff Lowell sighed and shook his head. He didn't seem surprised. "It's their church. That's Little Clementine for ya."

Jacinda adopted a flat-lipped smile that spoke volumes about how she felt about Little Clementine at this point. "That said, Sheriff Lowell and I have brainstormed finding a different home base. He's suggested the old community center we passed on the way into town."

"It's not ideal, or I would've suggested it to begin with." Lowell lowered his voice. "But it won't have the privacy headaches. You'll have electricity, and if we get some folks to assist in hauling over chairs..." He shrugged.

Leo bit his lip to keep from frowning. If electricity was a "benefit," that didn't bode well for working conditions.

Pastor Darl erupted from the base of the stairwell, his footsteps thumping on the basement carpet. "There's no reason for the agents to shift space!" He spread his feet as if ready for a physical fight. "Are you people running from the Lord? Because God will find you wherever you go!"

Jacinda placed herself between the pastor and the team.

Leo swallowed hard, his weak coffee loosening his tight throat. This so-called community leader had been listening to their every word since moment one. While chairs and electricity might be a low bar, Leo would trade running water for privacy at this point.

"Pastor Darl..." Sheriff Lowell walked up and placed both hands on the man's shoulders, separating him from Jacinda.

She let the sheriff take the pastor to the side, apparently thinking a familiar face in a uniform might do more good than a stranger Fed. Instead of intervening with the locals, she sipped her coffee, displaying the kind of cool that the Darls could only hope to emulate.

Beyond Jacinda and the pastor, Ian Darl emerged from the stairwell with an armful of cookie tins.

Leo rose to greet the newest bit of chaos. *Just what we need. Another person in clear sight of the murder board.*

"Dad, let's give these agents some privacy, all right? Calm down and let them do their work without giving them a sermon." Ian Darl gestured to the buffet of coffee and muffins with his tins. "Agents, I brought you some cookies, courtesy of my mother. If you think the muffins are good, you'll love—"

"These people don't need cookies." The pastor gripped his son's shoulder, a pinch too hard from the looks of it. "They need faith!"

Leo moved in behind Jacinda to assist if needed.

Whether the pastor accepted the change or not, they were moving base camp.

Pastor Darl shoved past his son, stepping farther into the room. Though he seemed content with yelling, Leo wouldn't have been surprised to see him start handing out prayer cards or waving a Bible. "No badge is more powerful than the will of God! Sheriff Lowell, you know this. How dare these agents not appreciate the generosity of our church."

Leo ignored the pastor. "Sheriff, can we take these chairs over ourselves? I'm guessing you can send a deputy to unlock the space for us?"

Jacinda hid a smile behind her untouched muffin.

Ian Darl seemed cowed by his father's loud protests.

The sheriff began making calls.

Near the crime board that Mia and Vance were already packing up, Jacinda waved for everyone's attention.

"We'll revisit the crime scenes today. I'm sure the sheriff's people searched them thoroughly." The SSA gestured toward the hubbub near the staircase. Diplomacy rang through her voice, not that the sheriff heard. "But both the Murray and the Crawford farms deserve another look, just in case. I also want to make sure we meet with the M.E. and start questioning citizens separately. There's too much solidarity among these people to trust that the full truth is shared when they're all gathered together."

Pastor Gregory Darl screamed over her. "You're threatened by the Lord's flock!" His voice trembled with anger. "Your fear only speaks of the deep and hidden evils within your own hearts!"

"Pastor Darl, I'm asking you to calm down." The sheriff faced off with the raving preacher.

The older Darl turned on the sheriff. "I demand you get rid of this outside intrusion and conduct the investigation yourself."

Poor Ian Darl stood off to the side holding the ridiculous stack of cookie tins.

Jacinda turned back to their team with a shake of her head and gestured with a twirling finger for them to wrap everything up. "Not another word. We will not say one more word in this building. Let's go."

With Jacinda leading the way, Leo grabbed two folding chairs in each arm and headed upstairs.

Not the way I expected to escape this old church, but I'll take it.

15

Though the windows were rolled all the way up, fending off the winter cold, the stink of animal feces invaded the Expedition when Mia and Vance were still a quarter mile from the Murray home.

Mia crinkled her nose as the smell grew stronger with their approach to the first murder scene. She parked just beyond the crime-scene tape roping off the farmhouse and immediate yard area.

Vance hesitated with his hand on the passenger door. "This stench is going to be worse outside, and I can already barely breathe." He scowled, took a deep breath of the cleanest air they'd have for the duration of their visit...and coughed.

Holding in a laugh, Mia waited for him to clear his throat. She opened her door and stepped out onto the driveway.

Off to the side, a cluster of maybe a dozen pigs rooted around in a giant mud pit corralled by weather-beaten fencing. An opening led from the corral into a small barn, letting the animals go in and out as they chose. The enclosure exuded the stink that filled the air.

A pig poked its nose between two slats of wood as if to investigate the newly arrived guests. It squealed like crazy, and a few others joined in. "Wonder who's taking care of them now? Some local, I guess? Must be a lot of work."

Vance had given up any sense of decorum, pinching the collar of his thick polo shirt between his fingers and pulling the fabric over his nose. "Whoever it is, they must not have a sense of smell."

As if for punctuation, Vance gagged—loud enough that a pig offered a snort in response—and Mia fought down laughter.

He's acting like such a poodle, the smell's almost worth the memory.

"Gear up?"

They grabbed their coveralls and stepped carefully through the sludgy yard. Mia wiped extraneous mud off her shoes and put on her Tyvek suit. The porch was the cleanest place to dress and prevent contamination.

Vance, sick of the outdoors apparently, fished out the key they'd been given by the sheriff first thing. He struggled with the lock, wiggling the key back and forth before finally turning it. "Lowell said the knob might stick. Apparently, the Murrays never really locked their door. Guess they thought the smell would keep intruders away."

By the time he opened the door, Mia lost the battle against her own snorts of humor.

He scowled at her.

She shrugged as he cursed under his breath.

"Gotta take humor where I can get it, all things considered." As Mia stepped inside, wondering how the couple survived the stench of their pigs, that mystery was solved as soon as Vance shut the door behind them.

The couple's home must've been well insulated. Calming fragrances accented the space. Lavender potpourri sat by the door to greet the agents. Through the doorway to the kitchen, mint plants and ferns hung from the ceiling.

Underneath the pleasant scents, however, there was a familiar, darker odor.

When they reached the bedroom where Ernie and Louise Murray had been slaughtered, Mia lost her smile. There was nothing humorous there.

Blood caked the sheets and headboard of the bed, with blood spatter reaching as far as the walls and floor. "Forensics still needs to take this. There shouldn't be this much evidence left in the room."

"Small sheriff's office. We'll message Jacinda when we're done." Vance hit the light switch by the doorway. The nightstand's homey lamp lit up the room as planned but was shadowed by blackened blood droplets that cast polka-dot-like shadows on the far wall.

Mia swallowed against her gag reflex. She'd seen ugly crime scenes before, but this one immediately ranked in her top five. "Guess this is why we're here, huh?"

Wordlessly, Vance pulled out two pairs of gloves and handed one to Mia. They poked around the bedroom first, peering into the drawers, the closet, and the rolltop desk by the window. The only notable find was that the window looked out over the pig corrals, suggesting the couple had really loved their hogs.

Farther down the hall, they searched the bathroom and the spare bedroom, as well as a linen closet and crawl space.

The kitchen was nothing more than a single couple's functional cooking area.

Mia shut the drawer she'd just rifled through. "Okay. So the front rooms and the kitchen don't appear to have been touched."

Vance leaned against the counter, crossing his arms. "The

front door wasn't kept locked. I think the killer just walked in."

"Bringing the murder weapon with him?"

Vance nodded. Picking up a nearby broom, he went to the front door where he stood on the threshold—without opening the door, Mia noted. Holding the broom like an axe handle, Vance continued his thought process. "Our perp makes it past the pigs without startling them into making a lot of noise."

"You can't really hear anything in here." Mia held a finger up to her lips. They were both quiet and listened. The house really was well insulated against both smell and sound. "Good construction."

Vance looked down at the welcome mat. "Think the killer got mud on his shoes? I don't see anything."

"Weather was cold for the Murrays, but dry. It snowed a little on the next night, with the Crawfords."

Her partner nodded to himself. "Okay. No tracks." Vance moved down the hallway to the bedroom. "It's the middle of the night, right? How dark would it be in here?"

Mia switched the lights out. They needed to get a sense of the situation as the killer would have found it...as much as they could at ten o'clock in the morning. Thin gray light shined into the living room space. Clouds obscured the sun. "It'd be pretty easy to see if the moon was out. Based on how much light we had last night, it was probably a near-full moon on the night of the murders. Killer could've seen outlines of furniture."

"It's pretty cluttered in here, though. The couch, the recliner, the end tables, television stand." Still wielding his broom-axe, Vance sneaked down the hallway. As he walked, they both listened for creaks in the floors. Nothing. "The killer doesn't necessarily need to know the space to move through it, but I think it's a good bet he knows the layout. I think he's been here before."

Mia nodded. "It makes sense. Nothing in the front of the house is disturbed. He headed straight back without hitting anything or stumbling or making noise."

They'd arrived at the bloody bedroom. Vance pointed with the broomstick. "Ernie Murray is closest to the bedroom door. It's just a couple steps and *wham*." Vance mimed lifting and lowering an axe.

"Wouldn't Louise Murray wake up?"

"She probably did. But look." Vance took another fake swing, showing how little stretch it took to reach the other side of the bed. "The bed's not that big. I think our guy swung at Ernie, taking him out first. Then he immediately struck Louise. After she was done, he moved back to Ernie and whaled on him for a while."

They stood in silence, soaking in the violence. Mia hated reliving it, but it was a necessary step to understanding what they were dealing with. "To sum up, this crime scene tells us, pretty clearly in my opinion, it was probably someone they knew. Looks like one of the 'flock' was furious with Ernie Murray, regardless of what the pastor says."

Vance leaned against the broom. "We've just got to get them to talk. I bet there're a lot of secrets here."

They returned the broom to the kitchen, turned out all the lights, and messaged Sheriff Lowell to have forensics come back in and do a more thorough job.

Standing at the front door, Vance scowled. "I wish we had a tunnel to get back to the SUV, but I guess we need to look around the yard while we're here."

Stepping outside, Vance gagged and yanked up his shirt through his Tyvek collar to cover his nose and mouth once more, but Mia couldn't laugh at this point. Not after the scene they'd confronted inside.

Even though the suit protected her shoes, she hopscotched her way around, as the thin material felt too flimsy to withstand the outdoors for long. Mia reached the barn ahead of Vance and unlatched the door. Inside, they were greeted by empty horse stalls and raked-up dung but nothing that might have been seen as suspicious or telling.

Vance high-stepped his path into the barn, keeping an eye out for any stray animal droppings. "Nothing but horse tack and farming tools and work gloves. *Nada*." He offered her a half grin. "I'm glad our second date could be in such a romantic setting."

Bless your soul, Vance Jessup, you are a romantic.

"I wasn't aware we were going on a second date, Agent Jessup."

He froze, one foot in the air, but her laugh gave away her true thoughts on the matter.

There wasn't much point in being coy when her poker face had deserted her.

When the barn door was shut behind them, Mia pointed to a smaller building near the tree line. "Crap. One more place to check."

He gestured gallantly, hiding his nose behind his shirt again. "Ladies first."

Mia sighed upon reaching the building. "Well, there's definitely a theme to this trip, and we can smell it and see it."

The outhouse door sported the typical crescent-moon cutout. It was run-down and, thankfully, no longer in use.

Mia pulled her shirt over her nose. The rancid smell of human discharge assailed them, impossible to ignore. Or breathe through. "This is gross."

Vance opened the door—ever the gentleman—and stepped back to let her peer inside. An ancient stack of *Playboy* magazines was piled in the corner. Ripped-out pages were tacked to the wooden walls.

"Oh, man." She shook her head and backed out of the doorway. "I think we just stumbled on Ernie Murray's spank bank."

Vance ducked his head into the outhouse before whipping himself back out, blushing like a preteen who'd just been caught by his mom. "Agreed. Seems like our Mr. Murray had a hobby he took pretty seriously."

Keeping her shirt over her nose, Mia stifled a laugh. "Time to go?"

Rather than answering directly, Vance started picking his way along the ground that separated them from their vehicle. He cursed when he stepped in something she didn't want to name.

She passed by as he kicked at the dirt. She unzipped her suit and threw it in the bag in the back of the Expedition.

Even with the Tyvek coveralls safely stored away, Mia could smell the farm coming off her clothes.

I'll have to throw my whole damn outfit away.

Behind her, the pigs snorted in what sure sounded like agreement.

16

It had to happen sometime. Might as well be today.
Ever since her ability to see and speak to ghosts had made itself known, Emma had bent over backward—inconspicuously to her colleagues, of course—to avoid visiting a morgue.

Aside from cemeteries, she couldn't imagine a less desirable location.

She could just picture it. A bunch of murdered people hovering around their hacked-up bodies. Their white-eyed faces staring at her. Some would threaten her. Some would beg her.

No way. No, thanks. Not if I can help it.

Her luck had run out, though.

Emma sat in the passenger seat as Jacinda drove to the Zeigler County Morgue forty-five minutes outside Little Clementine. As the county seat, Zeigler City, Maryland had been the automatic destination for their victims' bodies.

At least it got her out of Little Clementine for the moment.

Still, Emma could imagine the havoc. Dismembered

bodies walking around the morgue, scattering limbs everywhere. Heads popping out of cadaver drawers to speak to her. Some ghost hovering behind the M.E.'s shoulder, examining their own remains.

And the anger. If the ghosts of Heights of Glory Inn were any indication, she could be in for a lot of silent but undeniable anger.

Yay.

Emma realized she envisioned the morgue in zombie-movie terms rather than real life, but realistically, why shouldn't she?

Look at my life.

When Jacinda pulled up to the front of a surprisingly modern-looking hospital, snow blanketed the ground around the shrubs and parking lots. The asphalt and sidewalk were cleared and well kept. If Emma hadn't known better, she'd have thought the place was a university rather than a decades-old medical center. But that almost heightened her dread. Weren't horrors to be expected behind normal facades? At this point, it sure seemed like it.

Forcing herself to get out of the Expedition was an exercise in will, but Emma managed.

Jacinda leaned onto the main lobby's glass-fronted welcome desk. "We're here to meet the M.E., Jared Ankov. It's about the Little Clementine murders."

"Elevator is to the left." Though the lobby was otherwise empty, the woman barely looked at them. "Go down to the basement, and you'll find Dr. Ankov's office on the right... second door. Knock before entering. If he's not there, keep going down the hall, and you'll see the morgue."

Inside the elevator, Jacinda pressed the button for the basement and only spoke once the door closed. "You're quiet today. Everything okay?"

Emma forced a smile. "Just not looking forward to the

bodies." She forced some sympathetic bravado. "But someone's gotta be here for them."

"Too true."

The elevator dinged.

Jacinda led the way into the hall. Since her knock didn't bring Dr. Ankov to his office door, she followed the receptionist's instructions and headed farther down.

Emma inhaled a deep breath of the antiseptic air. Everything felt room temperature. No ghostly chills.

She shook her head. The ghosts would find her when they found her. She just needed to stay aware and not embarrass herself.

Jacinda knocked on the morgue door window, catching the attention of a blond man leaning over a desk station. He raised a hand, waving them in.

"Dr. Ankov? I'm SSA Jacinda Hollingsworth, and this is Special Agent Emma Last. We're here about the Little Clementine murders."

The man's blue eyes sparkled as he shook their hands. "You bet." For a medical examiner about to give them a tour of some bodies, he seemed awfully cheery. "Here are some gloves. You can use goggles and masks if you want. Grisly business. But if you'd told me we'd have an axe murderer coming from a small Appalachian town, I might've guessed it'd be Little Clementine."

He led them toward the cadaver drawers at the edge of the room.

Emma hurried to catch up, trying to ignore the sheet-covered body on a table nearby. The corpse wasn't a ghost, but still.

The sickly, cloying odor of death overshadowed the antiseptic smell, reminding Emma she hadn't enjoyed such visits even before ghosts started using her as their personal liaison.

"Uh, why aren't you surprised we're talking about Little Clementine?"

At the drawers, the man examined some labels and released a latch. Ankov turned back to them before he opened it, one hand on the drawer pull.

For the first time since they'd walked in, his smile seemed a bit forced—thin-lipped and polite rather than honest. "I'm Jewish. Little Clementine is decidedly unfriendly to outsiders, period. If you're not a Christian, and especially if you're not their particular type of Christian, their attitude goes positively arctic. I haven't spent much time there, but their reputation precedes them. Subservient women. Obedient children. Daily religious meetings. Arranged marriages. I've got a friend at the fire department who's told me stories that would make you think they're living in another century."

Jacinda pulled her iPad from her satchel. "So an axe murderer in the town isn't…surprising?"

The M.E. barked a laugh, light coming back into his eyes. "I hope an axe murderer anywhere outside of a horror movie will always be surprising. But those people are fanatical. They don't do anything halfway. Maybe it's just me, but I think a gun would be too impersonal for a citizen of Little Clementine. If someone deserved punishment in their eyes… I'm surprised these victims weren't beheaded in the town square."

Emma exchanged a quick glance with Jacinda. The doctor's words held the ring of truth—not just opinion, but fact. And that was worrying. His words described what Emma had been feeling.

Over the past thirty-six hours, she'd felt lost in a world of strange mores and traditions. She remembered Julianna standing behind her man, the pastor, her hand solidly on his shoulder, supporting him. Or the old pastor thundering on about fire and brimstone.

The morgue, with its reasonable M.E. and more modern technologies, seemed incredibly contemporary compared to what they'd experienced over the last day and a half. She felt like a time traveler who'd suddenly returned to the present.

"You sound as if you're convinced the killer is a member of the community," Jacinda observed.

Dr. Ankov nodded. "Hard to see how it could be an outsider. If you're asking my opinion, I'd say yes, it had to be someone on the inside. Someone who knew these people and had a deep-seated reason to want them dead. That's what we usually say about murders involving bladed weapons, isn't it? A crime of passion. Something personal."

The doctor wasn't wrong. Emma nodded. "It does seem that way."

Dr. Ankov pulled the drawer open. "A note on all the bodies..." The doctor adjusted his glasses, leaving the body sheet in place. "The initial drug tests have come back clean for all four victims. The rest of the test results won't be in for a week. I have no reason to believe any of the victims were seriously ill or incapacitated. I also have no reason to doubt they would have lived significantly longer lives if not for the murders."

What the hell? Emma raised an eyebrow. "An axe seems to make that pretty clear. They definitely would've lived longer if they hadn't been killed."

"Correct, but in such a religious community as devout in their fanaticism as Little Clementine is, I could see mercy killings being a possibility if the victims were seriously ill."

"Wouldn't they have chosen a less brutal method to provide a merciful death?"

"I'd like to think so, yes. But, like I've said, these people have their own ways, and they are vastly divergent from what most of society would consider normal."

The doctor pulled back the first victim's cover, stealing the air from the room.

Jacinda took a little step sideways, leaning one shoulder against the wall of drawers. "And this was no mercy or anything short of rage."

Ernie Murray's postmortem condition amounted to a puzzle the doctor hadn't quite managed to fit back together. Arms and head were all but severed from the torso. With cuts penetrating deep into various parts of his chest, Ernie's condition was most suited to a slasher film.

Even though someone had wiped Ernie clean of blood, his bare skin only highlighted the fact that there was no way to sanitize this amount of rage.

The Y-incision made for the autopsy was a papercut compared to what the killer had inflicted.

Dr. Ankov gave them a few seconds to process the body, then he pointed to the neck. "The fatal blow was to the neck. Based on the body's positioning when he was found and the closed eyes, I believe he was killed in his sleep. Meaning the first blow was also the killing blow."

"Small blessing." Emma leaned closer to the man's face, taking in the blank expression. "For what it's worth. That the killer went on to mutilate the body so thoroughly should put to rest any thoughts that this was done out of mercy."

"Indeed." The doctor directed their attention to the middle of the neck cut, where bone met muscle and tissue.

Emma's gut clenched, but she focused on breathing through her mouth and pretended the body was a dummy rather than a corpse. For her own sanity, if nothing else.

The doctor moved his gloved index finger close enough to the bone that it almost touched. "Note how the center of the cut is clean, even where the weapon hit the vertebral column and met real resistance. That speaks to the force of the blow, as well as the weight of the weapon."

Jacinda typed on her iPad, focused on her words more than the body. "Or the strength of the man?"

The doctor paused, pondering her question. "Possibly. I wouldn't want to speculate on the perpetrator's sex. Plenty of women can wield an axe. But look at the edges of the wound. The margins are less clean and regular than you'd expect from a smaller weapon, suggesting a heavy, thicker blade."

"So it's certain a knife wasn't used?" Emma asked.

"A smaller weapon…a knife of some sort or a hatchet rather than an axe, for instance…we'd see more signs of forceful pressure. Instead, we get these clean centers."

Emma swallowed hard. "Any idea of the type of axe?"

"I could be wrong, but I'd bet money the killer used a typical woodcutting axe. Something someone in a small mountain community like Little Clementine might keep around for chores."

"Are there any signs of debris in the wounds? Wood? Dirt?" Emma peered closer, despite wanting to move away. She didn't see anything, but the body had been washed down.

"No. The weapon must've been kept pretty clean and sharp." The doctor moved down the body to gesture to the centers of other wounds inflicted on the unlucky Ernie Murray, counting eight as he went.

Emma curbed the urge to count along with him like she was a character on *Sesame Street* by the end.

"And I take it the wounds on all the victims are similar in terms of weapon and force?" Emma followed him to the next drawer, which the doctor was just pulling out.

"They are, though the women didn't receive so many strikes, as I'm sure you already know. This is Louise Murray, forty-four years old and killed with the same weapon. We found her husband's blood inside her wound, which means the axe was still wet from his murder when the killer struck her."

Emma gazed down the body. Louise was cleaner than her husband, but that only emphasized her pale, grayish skin. "Was she...awake?"

The doctor grimaced. "I doubt it...I hope not. Her eyes were closed, but if you woke up to find your husband being victimized like this...?"

Emma swallowed hard again, trying to imagine the horror of watching a blade coming down. "I hope she was."

Dr. Ankov nodded, seeming truly affected by the gore for the first time since they'd entered the morgue. "There's added reason to believe she was asleep. Her husband wouldn't have had time to make a sound, dying with the first blow as he did. And since the killing blow was to the neck, there wasn't likely any cracking of bone. At least, not from that strike."

"But the later strikes?"

"It's hard to determine. The killer may have struck Louise immediately after her husband, ensuring she was also dead, and then finished the, um...task of mutilating his body. We found traces of her blood in his postmortem wounds."

Jacinda shifted her gaze from the body to the doctor. "I'm not seeing any defensive wounds, no damage to the hands as we'd expect if either of them had been conscious when the killer struck. So he killed them both fast, making sure they were unable to react. Then turned his attention to inflicting extra damage on the husband."

"That would be my conclusion. The next couple is a little different, but the overkill of the man is similar."

The doctor moved another drawer down and pulled out the third body of the day. "Chet Crawford. Close in age to

Mr. Murray. The initial blow killed him, but he received twelve postmortem wounds, four more than Ernie Murray."

Emma stopped herself from counting out the wounds. *Talk about unnecessary trauma.* Chet Crawford's body seemed almost ripped apart. The wounds looked like grotesque, gaping mouths.

Signaling they could keep going already, she moved to the other side of Chet after giving him a few respectful seconds. "And his wife?"

"The youngest victim." The doctor pulled out the next drawer and lifted the sheet to reveal twenty-six-year-old Rosemary Crawford. Her carrot-red hair gleamed glaringly bright under the morgue's lighting. An angry gash had been cleaned up on her right shoulder, where the killer's blade had nearly removed the flesh of her upper arm.

"She had a daughter?"

Emma forced herself to nod. "A two-year-old. She didn't appear to be touched."

After a second of silence, the doctor indicated Rosemary's neck. "I want to draw your attention to the difference in the neck hacks here. Look at where we have the uneven tearing of the skin compared to the other bodies. She was initially struck from the side instead of the front, like the killer was swinging a baseball bat. Then this second slice severed her cervical vertebrae between numbers four and five, killing her instantly. Though, of course, she would have died of blood loss without that blow."

Emma tried to imagine the scene, forcing herself to think only of the details and facts, not the very human trauma that would have played out in the moment.

"What can you determine about her positioning during the attack? That first slice almost makes me think she was standing up."

"I'd say you're right. She was almost certainly standing

upright when she was attacked. Probably facing her attacker. Then she fell, and the second and final blow was struck."

"Awake." Jacinda's whisper cut into the air. "Aware."

"Very much so, I'm afraid." A muscle in the doctor's jaw twitched, like he was holding back some emotion for the first time today. "Her eyes were closed when they found her, but whether the killer closed her eyes or Rosemary closed them when she saw the axe coming at her, there's no way to tell."

"What about any foreign DNA on the body?" Emma asked.

"We didn't find anything obvious, but we can assume the first victim's blood was present on the weapon. As I said, it'll take some time for trace tests to come back. I'll contact you as soon as they do. Meanwhile, I just hope the killings are over. I mean that. I wouldn't shed a tear if Little Clementine vanished from the map tomorrow. But not like this."

"Let's all hope." Jacinda shook her head, and the man pulled the cover over Rosemary before closing the drawer.

Emma found herself continuing to stare at Rosemary's closed drawer.

The men were so similar, but the women? There has to be a reason for the difference.

"If Chet was the primary target, and I think it's safe to assume he was, based on the overkill, I wonder…what if the killer meant to spare Rosemary? He let her daughter live. Maybe Rosemary, outside doing whatever she was doing, spotted the perpetrator, and he killed her out of necessity rather than desire."

"It's possible," Jacinda allowed. "Although, that doesn't fit with the two strikes to her neck, not when the first clearly would've done the job. And we still have no reason to believe Ellie Sue's survival wasn't just an oversight. If the child was sleeping, maybe the killer didn't think about her at all."

"But the blows are so violent and personal with the

men...we've been saying all along that the murders involved rage. That the killer probably knew the victims."

Jacinda crossed her arms, cradling her iPad against her chest. She nodded thoughtfully. "Which would mean he knew they had a daughter."

"Right. And the town is so small, the killer would know if the Crawfords dropped Ellie Sue off for overnights at her grandparents' house or something." Emma laughed a bit to herself. "Though it's not like there's a happening nightlife in Little Clementine. Unless prayer meetings and axe murder count."

Jacinda's usually steady demeanor broke for a moment. "Emma. Please."

"Sorry, SSA Hollingsworth."

"You can still call me Jacinda, but a little delicacy wouldn't hurt. Thanks for your help, Dr. Ankov." Jacinda waved farewell to the doctor, who had politely busied himself with closing the cold lockers while Emma was chastised.

He called over his shoulder as they departed. "Go get this bastard."

Jacinda led the way to the elevator. Emma could breathe easily for the first time since stepping into the morgue. Jacinda pressed the *up* button. "Okay, I'll buy that the killer spared Ellie Sue on purpose. She's only two. I've met plenty of hard-nosed killers who couldn't kill a toddler. Where does that get us?"

Emma flashed back to the almost peaceful expression on Rosemary's face. Her age compared to the other victims. The lack of extra blood...and her positioning outside.

They stepped into the elevator.

Emma pulled on her winter gloves. She began thinking out loud. "Rosemary's the real key here. The killer spared Ellie Sue. Rosemary's murder seems to have been spur-of-the-moment. A woman in the wrong place at the wrong time. If she'd stayed out of sight just a bit longer, she might not have been killed at all."

"Go on."

"I think this is mostly about the men." The elevator opened to the lobby floor as Emma continued. "But maybe Louise or Rosemary had something to do with why their husbands were targeted."

Jacinda held a finger to her lips as they walked through the lobby, signaling a pause in the conversation.

Outside, the SSA led the way to the SUV. "I buy that the men are central, obviously. But why target the women too?"

Emma hesitated at the Expedition's door, still trying to figure out the difference for herself. "I don't know. Maybe the killer was kinder to women because of some strange chivalry? Or maybe the killer related to, or sympathized with, the women somehow? He was prepared to kill everyone. So even if the rage is directed at the men, he had something against the wives too."

She climbed into the passenger side. Jacinda started the vehicle and hit the heater. Cold air shot into Emma's face, but it immediately heated up. Emma, likewise, warmed to her topic.

"So," Jacinda steered out of the parking space, "we're looking for a perpetrator with different levels of animosity or feelings for the separate victims. Rage against the men, some level of chivalry or sympathy toward Louise and Rosemary, and no animosity toward toddlers."

"Yeah, I think so." Emma flashed back to the doctor talking about beheadings, likening them to punishment.

Jacinda cut off her thoughts as she turned out onto the main road. "I want to congratulate you on working out that kind of insight in the face of such gruesome evidence back there, indelicacy notwithstanding. I'm impressed. In fact, I've been impressed by your work so far."

Emma blinked as her mouth dropped open, to the extent that Jacinda chuckled. "I...thank you."

"You've got to have more self-confidence. You're a talented agent."

Emma leaned back in her chair, smiling for what seemed like the first time that day. "But I'm usually shit at first impressions."

"I *have* noticed that." Jacinda gestured up ahead to a strip mall at the side of the road. "Think you can eat?"

Emma chuckled. "The others'll be jealous. We should probably bring them snacks."

She was about to say something more, but bit her lip instead when the realization struck her and sucked the breath from her lungs. Emma hadn't seen a single ghost all day.

Not even for a second.

And I've been in a friggin' morgue.

17

From the moment he'd entered the child's bedroom, Leo knew Ellie Sue Crawford's parents hadn't just loved her. They'd treasured the little girl.

A mobile swayed from the ceiling, so delicate that even Leo's slow movements around the room sent the toy animals spinning. Smiling whales and dolphins and seals drifted above the crib piled with pink blankets. The whole room was so lovingly decorated, in fact, the space could have been featured in a lifestyle magazine.

Antique wooden furniture. Perfectly placed stuffed animals. A playpen with just the right number of colorful toys. Cardboard picture books. Yellow walls sporting giant, decorative stickers—a smiling teddy bear sitting beneath a rainbow—near the large window seat.

The bear was probably the same size as Ellie Sue was now.

Aside from the master bedroom where Chet had been chopped up—which was awe inducing for the worst possible reasons—the house wasn't much to look at.

Yet the nursery was splendid. Any mother would've loved

to sit in the rocking chair and read to her child. The woven rug would be the perfect escape with some toys and a smiling toddler on a rainy day.

And Rosemary, at only twenty-six years old, had been ripped away from Ellie Sue's life with all the gruesome violence of a Wes Craven movie.

Leo released a loud sigh.

"You okay?" Denae hovered in the doorway. "You spot something?"

"Sorry, no." The sense of loss was almost overwhelming. "It's just so…ruthless. Seeing this room after the mess in the bedroom is a lot. The only thing I've spotted so far is tragedy. Ugly, senseless, permanent tragedy."

When Denae entered the room as well, she rested a hand on his shoulder for a second before moving over to the table by the rocking chair. She picked up a picture. The photograph showed a grinning child with bright-blue eyes and carrot-red hair. "Such a young child makes everything twice as dark, doesn't it?"

Leo scanned the floor, with its stuffed animals and wooden blocks, not trusting himself to answer. His eye caught on the floor vent in the corner. He'd barely given the grating a glance since it wasn't near any of the furniture, but now the anomaly glared at him, brighter than a spotlight.

The vent's grate was unsecured, propped over the hole it was supposed to be covering, four screws scattered around it.

That's not very safe for a toddler.

Adjusting his latex gloves over his Tyvek sleeve, Leo knelt beside the vent.

"What's up?" Denae shadowed him, standing at his side with the toddler's picture still in her hand.

"Why would you leave a vent uncovered in a baby's room?"

"You wouldn't."

"Exactly." Carefully, he pulled the grate away from the floorboards and reached inside, prepared for anything. Right away, his fingers touched a rubber-banded stack of slick paper. Polaroids.

When he turned them over and caught a glance at the first photo, his gut did a somersault. For a moment, he thought he might be sick. Instead, he rested one hand on the floor beside his knee, steadying himself before he pulled away the rubber band.

"Shit."

The top Polaroid showed a naked little girl, reclined on a couch.

Leo braced himself, teeth biting into his bottom lip, and flipped to the next Polaroid. This one had better lighting, and the girl's legs were spread. Maybe the same girl, or maybe not. No faces were shown, but that didn't make the pictures any less horrific.

From over his shoulder, Denae gasped. Leo turned to the next photo, then the next and the next, flipping through faster. As the pattern of the images was made more and more clear, his stomach roiled as rage seethed through his throat and stole his words.

No faces, but the naked girls were all young. Very young.

Hadn't graduated from grade school young.

Coming back to the first image, Leo replaced the rubber band to keep the sick collection together. He knelt on the floor a moment longer, disgust emptying his mind of anything else but the images he'd just been forced to take in.

He shoved the Polaroids into an evidence bag.

Though he couldn't quite tear his eyes up from the vent just yet, he stood. "We need to call Jacinda. Now."

18

Emma carried a fourth space heater into the community center Sheriff Lowell had provided. The sheriff was busy with crowd control outside, but between Emma and Jacinda, they were just about finished.

Inside, the others were finishing up a hurried lunch.

Electricity, running water, and space heaters. What more could a girl ask for?

Emma placed the last heater along the perimeter of the room before joining the rest of her team in the loose seating area they'd set up.

She joined Mia just as the other agent finished wiping her hands with a napkin. "I'm glad you and Jacinda brought food. How does this place not have a good burger joint? That's what those protesters should be protesting. Leave us alone. Go get food."

Emma laughed as she unzipped her coat and placed it around the back of her chair.

Despite Jacinda's best efforts, relocating to the run-down community center hadn't done much to discourage the citizens of Little Clementine. Most of them had simply followed the agents over, as if the FBI were a rock band and the citizens their groupies.

Technically, the SSA had the right to demand the crowd leave or face arrest, but Emma saw the sense in holding back.

Better to have the religious zealots on our side...or at least close by.

"Living the high life." Vance grabbed a seat on the other side of Mia. "With these fancy heaters, I feel like I'm back in college."

"The room does have that feel, doesn't it?" Emma shook her head, but the other half of her focus was on Jacinda as the SSA finished holding a quick phone conversation with the sheriff. Their impromptu briefing would be starting soon.

Lit by cheap fluorescents, the low ceiling appeared grimy and unstable. A small part of Emma kept expecting to hear rodents scurrying above. Although the meeting room had plenty of space, it was severely lacking in creature comforts.

The space heaters made everything either way too warm if they stood too close, or just short of wintery if they stepped outside the heat radius. Add the gruesome crime board, the lack of Wi-Fi, and the tacky floor tile that had been quickly mopped just for their benefit, and Emma wouldn't have been surprised to hear this was an old crime scene itself.

When Jacinda hung up and took her seat in the loose circle of chairs, she pointed first to Leo and Denae. "You two are going first. Emergency briefing officially in session."

Denae's eyes were lowered, and she seemed disinclined to speak. But Leo was ready with his iPad. Leaning forward, he pulled up images of the photos they'd collected and passed the device around the circle—strike one for lack of Wi-Fi—so that everyone had a glimpse, explaining how and where they'd found the Polaroids.

Emma was jolted when Leo had called her and Jacinda

earlier. Her mind buzzed with the idea that the murdered man—or couple, if that was even possible—had somehow been involved in child pornography.

Now, seeing the evidence firsthand, the ache of sadness in her chest was complete. The girls in the pictures weren't old enough to know the word "consent," let alone offer it. They were too young, in fact, to even really know that consent started with a C. They should've been watching cartoons after kindergarten and having snack time.

Vance updated their crime board with the new evidence.

Beside Emma, Mia fished out the tissues she normally kept for interview sessions and used one to dab her eyes.

"The pictures appear to have been taken at least somewhat recently." Leo set aside the iPad as it finished its circuit of the room. "There's no discoloration or yellowing present around the edges, so under a year easily, if not more recent."

Jacinda lifted her phone. "I spoke to the sheriff. He's already arranging for forensics to get over to the Crawford farm. They did a rough job in the bedroom, like at the Murrays'. They'll fingerprint the area around the vent where the pictures were found. But unless it's clean of foreign prints, we'll run on the theory these belonged to the Crawfords. We'll hear in the next few days if there's evidence to the contrary."

Emma eyed the crime board, where Vance still stood ready to write up any new developments or theories. "If Chet Crawford was involved in child pornography or abuse, then there's a clear potential motive for his death. A pissed-off parent or community member. Who'd know about it?"

And who'd be brave enough to do something about it? Outrage doesn't equal murder. Even in Little Clementine, where the rules all seem off the rails.

"Maybe this is another connection between the killings." Vance shifted in front of the board. "While it's not the same thing as child porn, not nearly, we've got a theme here. Mia and I discovered an outhouse full of pornographic images while we were at the Murray farmstead. Legally adult women, no question, and out of a printed magazine—"

"But that's still a pattern." Leo frowned, watching Vance as he noted down the find in "Ernie's Happy Place" on the board. "You said it was an outhouse. Did you check the hole?"

Vance frowned and turned back around to face them. "The *what?*"

Mia showed the same confusion as Vance, but Emma had been with Leo from the moment he'd spoken. "The waste hole. In the outhouse. Did you look inside it? Feel around for anything?"

Vance's nose scrunched, and his lips turned inward in disgust.

The expression was priceless, but Emma couldn't quite laugh, given the situation.

Mia shook her head. "That's…that didn't occur to us. The stench was, uh…"

"Prohibitive," Vance supplied.

"…and I guess we didn't even think about it. Sorry."

"No need to apologize." Jacinda stood and went to the board, starting a to-do list off to the side. "But I agree with Leo. It's worth a search. You two will need to go back and do a visual inspection."

Emma glanced sideways at Mia and mouthed, *Sorry*.

The other woman's lip quirked. Vance appeared about ready to lose his lunch.

Jacinda snapped her fingers twice to get their attention. "Focus, people. I know we need humor to survive, but we don't want this briefing to take all day. Meanwhile, if Chet and Ernie were both into child porn or sexually abusing young girls or both, the potential motive becomes clearer."

Mia thrust a hand into the air. "Jacinda, we've got indications that young girls in this community may have suffered sexual abuse. Excessive flirtation with older men, hints of promiscuity in how they present themselves."

"You mean the Sweeney daughters climbing all over Vance?" Emma asked.

Mia nodded. "I swear, one of them was ready to tear his shirt off and take a bite."

Vance slapped a hand over his face, but he didn't argue the point. "She's not wrong. Those two are trouble with a capital *T*."

Jacinda waved both hands to calm down the team. "Okay, people. We'll add that to the board. It may end up being relevant, or it may end up that Agent Jessup is too sexy for his job."

The whole group burst into a brief and welcome moment of hilarity but soon enough were back to business, running through their notes and trading comments about what they'd uncovered.

The photos Leo found were the most disturbing element Emma could think of, even more than the bloody axe murders. Exploiting an innocent child that way could absolutely inspire the kind of rage that would lead to explosive violence.

But that wasn't proven yet. Emma knew better than to trust what looked like an obvious answer when it came to catching a violent killer. The whole team knew better, especially after spending so much effort chasing the wrong person at the Ruby Red circus last week.

At least it's a connection, Emma girl. Small favors add up against evil.

Jacinda pointed at Mia and Vance, who'd sat back down. "Agents Logan and Jessup, revisit the Murray farm and finish what you started. I'm sorry, Vance. I know. Maybe bring an extra Tyvek or three. I also want the locals raked across the proverbial coals. Ambrose and Monroe, you two stay together and revisit Wade Somerson. He had a Polaroid collection of his own, right? Being the church photographer? Maybe he knows more about Ernie and Chet than he let on."

"Or," Emma pointed at Wade's name on the crime board, "he has his own pervert collection stashed somewhere. Just because he's still alive doesn't mean he's innocent. Of anything."

"I want everyone to give the board another look." Jacinda gestured toward the chalkboard with a chalk pencil. "Think for a second and see if we're missing anything. We've made a general victim profile, and now we need a profile on our perpetrator."

Emma nodded, waiting for her own assignment to drop. "And what do you want me on, Jacinda? Or am I with you?"

"Yeah, let's stick to the same teams for the day." Jacinda pulled some of her red hair through her fingers, combing the strands in a gesture that Emma was starting to recognize as an act of self-grounding. "We'll go over to the home of Bishop and Cora Hardy, Rosemary Crawford's parents. They weren't at the church yesterday…understandably so, considering they lost their daughter hours before…but we need to talk to them ASAP. Aside from any insight they have on Rosemary, they may know something about Chet and Ernie."

Mia picked up a pencil and added Bishop and Cora Hardy to the to-do list on the board. "In a town this size, someone has to know something."

"Or everyone knows everything but is saying nothing." Emma stood and picked up her coat as Vance went around the room to turn off the space heaters.

Mia joined him. "Maybe one of them will grow a conscience."

Emma hoped Mia was right and that one of these people

had a conscience they could exploit. She was more than ready to start digging into the minds of the forty-three citizens still left alive in Little Clementine.

It wasn't as if she could ask the dead, after all. The Other and its inhabitants seemed to have all but abandoned her.

I should be so lucky.

"They'll probably show up when I'm trying to sleep." She hadn't meant to whisper that thought, but Leo gave her a sideways glance.

"Huh?"

"Nothing. Just anxious to get going."

He nodded, turning back to focus on the board. Emma allowed herself a silent gush of relief, though her throat had dried up entirely.

Even with the ghosts gone, I'm still on the edge of making myself look as confused as a cross-eyed duck. Lovely. Just lovely.

19

Bishop and Cora Hardy had one of the statelier homes in Little Clementine, with a spacious wraparound porch and a stone walkway lit by a half dozen lamps. The day was so cloudy that the automatic evening lights were already on. Their eerie yellow shine on the walkway somehow made the path to the front door even gloomier.

On another day, Emma would've wanted to curl up with a friend on the porch swing and order pizza. Today, the idea of food turned her stomach.

Polaroids like those at the Crawford farmstead could do that.

The hanging *Welcome* sign jangled as the door opened, revealing a man in his fifties who was so gray, he could've easily passed for a ghost. At his shoulder hovered a slightly younger woman, clutching Ellie Sue like the little girl might disappear if she dared to let her go for even a moment.

Emma couldn't blame the woman, considering what had happened to her daughter.

The couple had been waiting for them.

"Mr. and Mrs. Hardy, I'm Supervisory Special Agent

Jacinda Hollingsworth, and this is Special Agent Emma Last. We're in town investigating the recent murders, including your daughter's." Jacinda left off there, waiting for the invite inside, and Bishop obliged with a vague gesture.

Leading them into a spacious living room, the couple chose seats beside each other in two matching armchairs. The orphaned toddler in Cora Hardy's arms smiled at Emma around her pacifier. Emma smiled back, but her stomach ached for the little girl.

At least she had her grandparents and was too young to know what was happening.

Maybe by the time she's old enough to understand, they'll have figured out how to tell her. Miracles happen, right?

Jacinda leaned forward from her perch on the couch, clasping her hands in front of her. "You have our sincerest condolences. We have some questions, but how about we start with you telling us anything that might be pertinent to our investigation? Anything you think might have driven the recent murders or attracted a killer to your daughter and her husband?"

Bishop's Adam's apple bobbed as he swallowed. But he remained quiet while his wife answered.

"I don't know what kind of monster is capable of…that. Why my baby girl?" Cora clamped one arm tighter around the toddler. She reached out her free hand to grip her husband's. "I think there's no question who did this. Wade Somerson was the last person to see both families. I always thought he lusted after my sweet, young Rosemary once his wife was laid in the ground. Grace was a godly woman, but I've had my doubts about Wade."

More than grief, anger lit Cora Hardy's eyes. Anger like that, directed at a man her community described as more pitiful than capable, struck Emma as reactive rather than objective.

"Doubts?" Emma prodded.

"You agents need to be talking to him." Cora bounced the toddler, perhaps a little harder than necessary. Ellie Sue's head bobbed. "I've heard from other folks that Wade has nobody on God's green Earth to vouch for his whereabouts. What do you say about that? What more do you want?"

She tightened her hold on her husband's hand, and Bishop finally gripped hers back...but he shook his head at the same time.

"Cora, honey." He turned to his wife, ignoring the agents. "You've always thought every man was lusting after Rosemary since the girl turned ten."

Emma wondered why Cora would worry about adult men lusting after her ten-year-old. Unless Chet Crawford's photography collection wasn't so secretive, after all. That thought put Emma on edge.

Did Cora know about those photos and know the girls in them?

Bishop's hand fell from his wife's, and her face darkened, going from pale to purple almost instantly. Her next words confirmed Emma's first impression. "Some men aren't as godly as they claim. Did you know Wade Somerson banished his son? Sent him off to reform school."

"Do you know why?" Emma tried to keep her face and body movements neutral. Cora seemed incredibly on edge, which Emma understood from an intellectual standpoint. Violent deaths were traumatic to process, even for professionals. Asking a loving, grieving mother to stay calm was almost impossible.

Bishop shifted in his seat. "I've known Wade since grade school, and I just can't see the man being capable of murder." He kept his focus on the agents, ignoring whatever his wife muttered under her breath. "I'll be honest. I know we married Rosemary off to Chet, a man twenty-two years her senior. It was a decent marriage, and I think she was happy, especially when Ellie Sue came along, but…" He glanced at his wife.

"It was an arranged marriage. As if this were the Dark Ages. As if we should trade our daughters for two sheep and a half acre. As if…" Cora all but quaked with fury as she ran out of examples. The baby let out a little whimper.

Bishop stood and plucked the child from his wife's arms, taking her over to a fancy playpen in the corner.

Emma was glad. She'd feared the woman would bob the child into a concussion if her color went much higher. As it was, Cora's cheeks were nearly neon violet as she went on. "We married her to someone old enough to be her father."

"Enough, Cora." Bishop didn't raise his voice, but there was something in his tone that reminded Emma of her father when he was in a very foul mood. She even experienced a small quiver in her stomach, as if her dad had just reprimanded her for low grades.

Cora quieted, but Emma sensed it was a hard thing. The self-control the Little Clementine women demonstrated was impressive, if frustrating. She wondered what Cora or the pastor's wife or Lizbet Somerson would tell them if they were separated from their husbands for even fifteen minutes.

Emma forced a smile, trying to keep the moment as pleasant as she could. "And why Chet Crawford, if you don't mind my asking?"

Bishop sat down beside Cora once more. "They were a good pair. Certainly, it was hard for them at first. But love had to be there for our Ellie Sue to arrive."

Emma didn't point out that there didn't need to be love for there to be babies. "And?"

"Cora's grieving, but that doesn't change what Rosemary and Chet had. Chet had never found himself a wife, and Rosemary's childbearing years were passing her by. Everybody knew, of course, that she was waiting for the pastor's son to ask for her hand, but Ian Darl has a greater calling." A small snort escaped Cora, but Bishop ignored her. "Ian admitted as much. He's married to the word of God, and we all respect him the more for it."

Emma examined the pinched expression on Cora Hardy's face. "How well did you know Chet Crawford when you agreed to the marriage? In a town like this, I imagine he asked for permission?"

Bishop's brow furrowed. "What kind of question is that? Yes, of course he asked our permission, like any respectable man would. We were glad to give it. We've known Chet our whole lives. What are you getting at?"

His wife couldn't bottle her words any longer. "What did Chet do? Did he go and do something that got my daughter killed?"

"Chet was a good man who believed in God." Bishop took a deep breath. He managed to maintain his calm better than his wife. "The monster who killed them did so without cause, I'm sure. Some sort of deranged stranger."

Ellie Sue whimpered in the corner, drawing Bishop from his chair once again to comfort the child. He picked up a music box plushie.

Emma met Jacinda's eyes ever so briefly as "Twinkle, Twinkle, Little Star" began to play. It wasn't clear whether the Hardys had a clue as to Chet's probable perversions. But they weren't going to learn anything with the pair together.

Jacinda stood as Bishop rejoined them. "Would you be willing to talk to us separately for a moment? It won't take long."

"I'm afraid Ellie Sue is fussy. We're happy to talk to you more, but I think we'll have to do it at a later time. We're done here."

A muscle in Jacinda's jaw twitched. Emma knew she was just as furious at the dismissal as Cora was at her daughter's death. But Jacinda accepted Bishop's reasoning for the moment. "You have our sincerest condolences." She gripped his hand. "And I promise we'll do everything we can to bring justice for Rosemary."

"You'll arrest Wade Somerson, then?" Cora gripped Jacinda's hand next, but she didn't let go so easily as her husband had. "And put him in jail to suffer? He can't be left to live free after what he did."

"I have a pair of agents speaking with Mr. Somerson. If he is responsible, we'll certainly pursue prosecution. In the meantime, everyone is innocent until proven guilty. We'll investigate as thoroughly as humanly possible." Jacinda patted Cora's hand and leaned closer to the woman. "God will bring to light what is hidden in darkness."

"First Corinthians 4:5. One of my favorites." Cora seemed to relax for the first time since they'd walked in the door.

"Indeed." Jacinda tugged her hand away.

Emma, once again, found herself admiring her new SSA. Jacinda managed to read any room she walked into.

As Emma inched toward the door, Bishop Hardy wrapped his arms around his wife, who was now crying quiet tears. Back on the walkway, Emma had to work to slow her step so she wouldn't slip on the frosted stone.

She'd been anxious to get back to questioning people when the team was working the case at the community center. They'd found what looked like leads and likely avenues to pursue, and they all pointed toward members of the community. But the sight of that orphaned toddler had broken something in Emma's chest.

"You were very kind to Cora. I don't know if I could've been."

Jacinda shook her head as they walked, her voice barely carrying over their footfalls. "Those poor people have no idea who they married Rosemary to."

Emma slowed her pace even more. "Cora might've had an inkling. What's worse is that no one may ever know if Rosemary did or didn't know about Chet's sickness. Even if the people of Little Clementine are as interconnected as a damn crossword puzzle, they're all wearing blinders concerning their 'upright' and 'God-fearing' neighbors."

Jacinda sighed. "Amen."

Emma could only swallow a dark laugh at her boss's ironic use of the affirmation. As the SUV roared to life, taking them back to the community center, she glanced out the window through the gray fog of the day.

Bishop Hardy stared back from the house's front window as they pulled out of the driveway, more ghostly than anything Emma had seen from the Other.

20

"I feel like I'm going to be thanking you for this one for a long time, Agent Jessup. You're a true gentleman." Mia meant every word she said.

Despite his clear preference for not having to perform the additional search at all, Vance had gallantly insisted on being the one to examine the waste hole for any hidden goods. Mia was quick to accept his offer. He'd worn three sets of plastic gloves and wrapped black garbage bags tight around his arms on top of a fresh Tyvek suit. Even with the respirator, he gagged the whole damn time, but he managed.

He shined his flashlight into the pit.

The seat—thankfully a typical toilet seat—lifted on dirt-encrusted hinges. Mia held her breath as Vance leaned low, his head sinking into the hole. Beams of light shot out occasionally as he moved around.

"It's pretty deep. Ugh. Shreds of toilet paper. Lots of, um, mud."

I sincerely hope it's mud but know better.

Mia stood in mute solidarity beside her fellow agent, not

wanting to shake Vance's determination. Until she could no longer take it.

"Anything else?"

Another stream of flashlight movement answered her. "Nope."

Part of her wondered whether he was more disgusted at not finding anything. At least the alternative would give him something to show for his efforts.

Vance surfaced, managing to remove his head and stand upright without having to lean on the toilet seat or bench. "We've done our due diligence. Let's get the hell out of here."

They moved to the Expedition at a fast clip, Mia giving Vance a wider berth than normal.

"I'm just thankful I thought to have a change of clothes in the SUV." He hauled off his respirator and Tyvek suit, which he stuffed into a trash bag. Next to come off was his baby-blue polo shirt, which he tossed onto the ground before rubbing hand sanitizer across his torso, neck, and arms. Though Vance didn't seem concerned about the icy January air, goosebumps sprung up along his bare skin.

Mia turned to respectfully give him a moment, but allowed herself a quick, admiring glance of his abs. From the corner of her eye, she watched him throw on a long-sleeved button-down and his FBI jacket.

Vance kicked the discarded polo farther away. "I don't think I can wear it again."

"You're gonna leave it?"

"The pigs can have it."

The drive back to the community center was uneventful, but Vance still needed to park as far from the crowd of citizens as he could without being outside the parking lot. The number of protesters—or maybe they were just curious onlookers—hadn't decreased.

Oddly enough, the town hadn't seen any major media presence yet. A few journalists roamed among the gathered townspeople, but nobody seemed inclined to answer any questions. Mia recalled what the sheriff had said about the people of Little Clementine preferring to keep everything quiet.

Exiting the SUV, Mia schooled any remaining humor from her face and pointed toward a woman at the edge of the crowd. Wearing a long black coat and sporting prim kitten heels, even in the winter weather, she was just the woman Mia had been hoping to find here.

"There's Julianna Darl. You mind running interference while I try to get her alone?"

"Call me your personal fullback. Defending against outhouse stenches and fanatical pastors, whatever may come your way."

"Can you possibly use those outhouse superpowers to distract the good pastor?"

Vance shot her a quick smile before separating from her as they reached the crowd. Waving one sanitized arm, he drew the pastor's attention, forcing the man to turn away from his wife.

"My hero." Mia's mutter went unheard, but the play had been called.

She reached Julianna Darl and caught her by the elbow, leaning close with a friendly smile. "Julianna, I was hoping to find you here. Can we chat real quick? Okay, great, let's just go inside for a few minutes…"

Mia babbled on as she guided the pastor's wife into the community center.

The deputy on watch stood just within the door, hogging the heat from the single space heater still left on.

Mia nodded for him to go outside and mouthed a *thank-you* as she guided Julianna to one of the chairs.

"Let's just sit here and get warm while we chat. That would be fine, right?"

Julianna's words of protest faded at the warmth from the space heater. She pursed her lips as she looked back out at the cold gray afternoon. Her brown eyes reminded Mia of a doe's—soft, pliant, but with a hint of skittishness. "I guess so. My husband and I always—"

"Can we talk about you, Julianna? Everyone in town has so much respect for your husband…we've heard a lot about him and from him. I'd love to hear from you."

"My husband and I are together in all—"

"I know, and it's so admirable." *Gimme a break, lady.* "But if you could just tell me your thoughts on what's happened, I'd so appreciate it."

Though Julianna was taking off her gloves and holding her hands out to the space heater, which seemed like a good sign, she frowned. "Yes, I know you want to hear from everyone, but my husband and I—"

"Don't have the same mind or experiences." Mia gripped the woman's knee maybe just a touch too hard. "You're a smart, independent woman who just happens to be married to a wonderfully religious man who's a pillar of your community. I imagine you must be a leader in your own right."

The woman simpered, lowering her head in what Mia thought was a nod.

Man, she's making me lay it on thick.

Mia patted her knee, channeling her inner patriarchy. "But I know he respects you enough to want you to speak on behalf of…on behalf of your God-fearing community. Right? You can do that for me? I just want to get your viewpoint, your own opinion, so I have the full picture. A woman's perspective means so much. Pretty please?"

The woman frowned at her hands as she held them out

toward the heater, rubbing them together as if twirling Mia's words between her palms.

For a second, Mia thought her overly friendly vibes hadn't broken through. Until the woman finally sighed and sat back in her seat.

"I want your team to do God's good work in finding justice."

Thank you, thank you, thank you.

Mia hid a sigh of relief and released the woman's knee. Maybe they'd get somewhere after all. "Okay, so let's start with who you think might've been capable of this."

The woman's brown eyes darkened. "Agent Logan, this was the work of a monster. I don't believe anyone in Little Clementine is capable of these violent murders..."

Mia couldn't believe her luck. She sensed a *but* coming. "But?"

The woman pressed her lips into a deep frown. "But, as a woman of faith, I also must allow that Judas was one of the twelve apostles, and he still betrayed Christ."

Okay. What am I supposed to do with that?

"And...?"

Emotion clogged up Julianna's voice. "This isn't how the world is supposed to be. This isn't who the people of Little Clementine are."

Mia fished out a tissue and pressed it into the woman's shaking fingers. She gave Julianna a few seconds to gather herself, then pushed while she had the woman's attention. "How well did you know Chet Crawford?"

Julianna shrugged, her gaze focused back on the little space heater. "Chet was devoted to God. He followed his pastor's guidance to the word. He was gifted with a young, beautiful wife, to whom I can only imagine he was very attentive. And blessed, of course, with little Ellie Sue." Not even a hint of dishonesty resounded in the woman's words.

"And has anyone in the congregation ever stood out as possibly being just a little bit more unstable than the rest? I'm sure," Mia hurried to speak over the oncoming protests, "that a pastor's wife would notice such a thing. You're basically the mother of the entire town, right?"

If Mia hadn't been watching so closely, she would've missed Julianna Darl's breath catch on the question.

When she parted her lips a second later, Mia was certain the woman was going to speak a name—or names—but instead she lowered her eyes.

When Julianna Darl met Mia's gaze again, she'd adopted her falsely cheery expression. "I notice everything. As a mother, I take care of my children as best I can. I have responsibilities." There was no truth to the woman's smile now. Julianna offered only the rote answers of those toeing the party line.

"Julianna...please. Can you—"

"My husband and I have told you and your team everything we can to help, I'm afraid." The woman smiled, reapplying lip balm before slipping her hands back into her gloves. "But perhaps you and your colleagues would like to join us for a church service tomorrow night, should you still be in town? You'll understand just how pure Little Clementine is, how wholesome the people are. And maybe...maybe some of the Lord's light will shine upon you too."

21

Leo had already ordered the least healthy thing on the menu at Abraham's Country Pan, Little Clementine's only restaurant, tucked around the corner from the motel. Despite the day they'd had, he couldn't resist his stomach's urging, so he plucked up another buttered dinner roll and shoved half of it into his mouth at once. Real food was real food.

The harried owner was cooking solo, so he'd peppered the team's table with baskets of bread to hold them over.

And just as advertised, the rolls were melt-in-your-mouth, butter-laden fantastic, and pillowy too. They almost made up for the day.

Almost.

Denae used her third roll to gesture to the half-empty bread basket between them. "Hard to leave room for dinner, huh? Or are you eating your frustration?"

"I just hate how useless today turned out to be." He caught Emma raising an eyebrow at him—he'd spoken too loudly—and lowered his voice so the other restaurant patrons didn't overhear. "We should've found something. Maybe if we could've gotten into Somerson's place again…"

Leo scowled and filled his mouth with another chunk of dinner roll.

When he and Denae had cruised back to Wade Somerson's house, not a soul had answered. Leo's knuckles went red from the cold and from knocking repeatedly before he'd finally given up.

The frustration of having been given permission to search, then not being able to do so again, had just about driven him insane. He even considered entering the photographer's home despite his absence.

Denae had logicked some sense into him before he could ruin the entire investigation, reminding him that they had nothing to prove. Somerson had given them his blessing before, which meant if they broke in and found evidence or received a complaint, and Somerson denied ever having given permission, they'd be screwed.

We must've missed something. Maybe he wasn't home because he expected us to come back.

Beside Leo, Mia tapped her phone. "It's six thirty already. What time do you think we're eating?"

"Soon." Vance sighed from across the table while staring at his phone. "Give the guy a break. He's the only one here."

Farther down the table, Emma had the best sight of the kitchen. "It's coming. I can smell the butter now. Practically taste it. Delicious."

"Ha." Leo leaned back, peering toward the kitchen. He was grateful Jacinda suggested they come to Little Clementine's one restaurant for a "think tank" meal. While the vast majority of the town's citizens were holding a prayer vigil from five to ten o'clock, the team had free reign of the place. Jacinda, of course, had wanted them to attend the vigil, to observe and gauge reactions among the townspeople. But the good Pastor Darl had insisted his flock "be left to conduct their worship in peace." Not wanting to ruffle the man's feathers any more than she already had, Jacinda agreed. But only for tonight.

With my luck, the next time they hold some kind of vigil, Jacinda'll ask me to lead them all in prayer.

After returning to Somerson's place, with no luck, he and Denae had spent the whole afternoon questioning various locals, trying to get a sense of whether the community had any knowledge of Chet's extracurricular activities. Or Ernie's pinup-girl fetish.

They'd had no luck at all, which meant the only thing they'd accomplished that day was finding the Polaroids.

"Dinner is served!" The owner edged out of the kitchen with a huge, loaded tray, approaching at a faster pace than Leo would have deemed safe.

His mouth watering for more than bread, Leo watched the man parcel out their meals. Abe had kept the restaurant open by himself that evening just for their benefit, and by all appearances, the chef knew his way around a kitchen.

Barbecued ribs landed in front of Mia and Vance, with sides of corn on the cob and salad crowding the space beside them. Denae's crab cakes were the house specialty, oversized and crispy. Jacinda and Emma were awarded with plates of baked chicken, fresh squash, and roasted sweet potatoes.

Arguably, Leo'd gone the least healthy route of all, but the dish left him nothing to complain about. An oversize pork chop took up most of his plate, gravy included, with mashed potatoes slathered in more gravy and green beans with caramelized onions on the side.

"Watching your cholesterol, huh?" Denae gestured to Leo's plate with a knife.

He grinned and dug into the main course. Closing his eyes, he sighed in satisfaction. The meat all but melted in his mouth, and although he wouldn't have admitted it to anyone, the gravy on the potatoes was better than his Yaya's recipe.

"This is what I'm talking about." Denae dug into her crab. "Nobody does crab cakes like a small-town restaurant."

No team member replied to her with words. Instead, nods and grunts of satisfaction sounded their universal agreement.

The plan had been to wait for the food to arrive before talking about the case, once there'd be no fear of Abe walking over at the wrong moment, but with meals in front of them, plans had changed.

Little hums of appreciation and the clicking of utensils offered the only noises around the table until Mia eventually gave in to her barbecue sauce and hurried from the table to request more napkins.

Leo bit into another piece of perfectly crisp green bean, then sipped from his water.

I'd kill for an ice-cold lager to wash this down with right now. Or two. Ten, maybe.

Abraham's Country Pan was, of course, a dry restaurant. The Prohibition days might as well never have ended in the little town. Maybe that was for the best, though.

Axe murderers and inebriation probably wouldn't make for the most awesome of combos.

Mia finished her meal first—apparently the ribs had, true to their advertisement, been of the best fall-off-the-bone variety. She ripped open the little package of disposable hand wipes that accompanied her dish. "So now that we've had our bellies filled, who's ready for some entertainment?"

Across the table from her, Vance scowled. Clearly, the man knew what was coming and wanted no part in it.

"Please tell me you've got a bottle of wine hidden in your purse." Emma pulled some chicken from the bone on her plate. "Or tell me you solved the case, and we can get back to D.C. in time for a show?"

Mia rolled her eyes. "Funny. But you're not all that off base about the show part of that theory. When I spoke to Julianna Darl today, she invited all of us to attend Pastor Darl's church service tomorrow night."

Leo froze with a piece of pork chop halfway to his mouth. "You can't be serious. There's no way in Hell, or Little Clementine, I'm going to one of that joker's sermons." All day long, he and Denae had suffered the stares and biting, half-whispered comments from the townsfolk. What should've been obvious—that the team's religion had no bearing on the case—had instead been understood as rude manners at best, and as a sort of failing at worst.

And it hadn't helped their investigation at all that 'most everyone they talked to was more content to proselytize than to provide any genuine answers.

Vance balled his napkin and tossed it to the middle of the table.

Denae focused on the remains of her meal rather than bothering to respond. Always calm and reasonable, that one.

Emma tapped her fork thoughtfully on her otherwise cleaned-off plate. "I mean...not that we want to attend, and not that we'd actually participate, so to speak, but as for just going for the event? It's not the worst idea, assuming we haven't solved the case by tomorrow night. Seeing one of Darl's sermons and how the town reacts could prove enlightening."

Jacinda was nodding.

Dammit to all hell.

"Emma's right." Jacinda sat back in her seat as she loosened her coat. "As long as we stay impartial and don't engage, and as much as I don't want to subject us to more of Darl's antics unnecessarily…us going couldn't hurt. If we keep our eyes peeled and our guards up."

Vance couldn't keep his disgust to himself any longer. "This is worse than sticking my head down a shithole."

Jacinda ignored him. "All right, then that's our plan." Jacinda pushed her plate forward, stacking side-dish plates atop it. "If you're not done, keep eating, but let's get this think-tank meeting started. Denae, how about you start, since you've already cleared off your crab cakes?"

Leo popped another green bean into his mouth as his partner recounted the day's events. The plan to attend the service made sense, but what made his throat itch, urging him to protest, was that the church simply creeped him out. Duty bound or not, he didn't want to attend a church service…least of all one in Little Clementine.

Finishing his food as Denae wrapped up her short summary of their afternoon, Leo once again wished he had a beer to sit back with. The rest of his team likely felt the same as he did about being stuck in the bizarro small town.

He sighed, tuning in to Mia's summary of her mostly unproductive chat with the pastor's wife.

"Ya know," Denae leaned toward the middle of the table and lowered her voice, "all things considered, maybe we should take a shortcut on this case and dress up as angels for the service. Somebody'd talk to us then, right?"

For a moment, Leo pictured Denae dressed up in a choir robe with fake wings and a yellow halo of pipe cleaners dancing above her curls. He laughed, feeling himself relax a little.

Across from him, Denae grinned in satisfaction.

There are worse ways to spend an evening than with this team, at least.

Getting hacked into pieces by a maniac, for example.

22

I kept the axe low just in case Bud peered out a window. Odds were, the old man was probably asleep...but better safe than sorry.

The Lord helps those who help themselves.

Creeping closer to the trailer, I drifted toward the old oak in the yard, keeping my boot treads to the path under the big shade tree. That was the key, to make sure my footsteps drifted right along with everyone else's littering the guilty man's yard. Not that my boot tracks would stand out from most others in town, and not that these were my boots, but caution came first.

Taking Ernie Murray and Chet Crawford out of this world was righteous and good, but killing Bud Darl is going to be pure ecstasy.

The axe hung against the side of my leg, its weight like the pull of God's own fingers around my heart. My shoulders might have been sore, but I would find the strength. He was with me in this moment.

God would enjoy this part of the plan as much as I would.

I whispered to Him His own words from Romans 12:19.

"'Rather give place unto wrath: for it is written, Vengeance is mine; I will repay, saith the Lord.'"

Nobody in Little Clementine deserved to be hacked to pieces more than Bud Darl.

Violent, self-righteous, physically and verbally abusive to the men and women he called his own family. He was a godforsaken pervert who fully believed he was going to live out his disgusting life without ever having to answer for all those little girls.

To think I'd believed his preachings when I was young. Believing in duty, obedience, and man's domination.

Bud Darl was as corrupt and depraved as any man on God's green Earth.

I had to lean against a tree, staggered by the evil lying in the trailer ahead of me.

How many nights had I prayed to forget that one conversation I'd overheard years ago?

God made me remember it, for nights like this, so I'd follow His plan.

So I'd understand what had to be done now that my path was clear. So much had been taken from me in this town. The guilty would not leave me bereft of hope.

I'd been under this very shade tree. Once upon a time, there'd been a swing hanging down from a branch. Nearly every child in town had played on the swing at one point or another. I now understood Bud had used the swing to lure kids in.

I'd pushed friends on that swing myself, laughing.

Now I can't remember the last time I laughed.

A few years back, the rope had broken and not been replaced, but a sense of joy still lingered around this tree.

Until I understood what—who—the swing offered up to the old sinner.

For me, the joy had been destroyed on a summer night

when Bud, Gregory, Chet, and Ernie had been playing cornhole out behind this trailer. The men drank Ernie's moonshine, which he made in the backwoods behind his farm.

With the weight of the axe in my hand, the memory was more incentive than torture. I remembered every devil-driven word of what those men had said, reliving their so-called "glory times" of all things.

All the time, thinking they were alone. Then, like now, I stood invisible.

I'd come to Pastor Bud's on some errand…

I could practically taste the moonshine on my tongue, as I'd been plied with it several times before. It'd made me sleepy, and after visiting the pastor, I'd made my way home.

But I must have passed out, because I remembered waking up with my head resting against this shade tree's trunk.

Somewhere close by, Bud Darl's cackle assaulted the night, over and over, drunk and full of fire. At first, I'd thought to follow his voice, as I'd been taught to do when I was a child.

My parents had taught me right. The pastor's voice was the voice of grace in Little Clementine. "You'll always be safe with a man of God leading the way."

But what I heard the pastor saying that night was anything but graceful, and as far from godly as could be imagined.

"Boys, you'll never know the thrill I had as a young pastor. All that power." Bud crowed into the night as a beanbag hit the wood of the cornhole board. "All that young, tight flesh to myself. Man alive, no red-blooded, God-fearing American would have turned it down, not in a month of Sundays."

Ernie's voice pierced the night, slurring from the moonshine. "Bud, we all know you're exaggerating. Leastways a little. People in this town—"

"Hold your tongue," Bud Darl boomed, then paused for effect, just like in one of his sermons.

My guts cramped, like when I was a kid on Sunday.

I already felt sick from what little I'd heard. I ought to run away from the trailer, maybe even far away from Little Clementine, but I couldn't make myself move.

And then Bud went on. "Boys, I tell you, I barely let one day go by without blessing one of Little Clementine's youth with my seed!"

More beanbags hit the cornhole board, thudding on the wood with little oomphs of glee as Gregory, Ernie, and Chet laughed along.

One of our community mothers had spoken to me of the rumors. Young girls waking with mysterious bruises. She confided that her twelve-year-old had woken the other day with strange bleeding. What was she to do?

I'd explained it away. It could have been an odd menstrual period, early and short. The pain explained by normal monthly causes.

Yet the dark rumors were true.

I'd dug my nails in deep, bracing myself against the evil going on just yards away.

Tears came fast on seeing the blood from the unintentional self-harm, and I bit my lip hard.

The men were still laughing. Ernie passed around photos, Polaroids.

Bud Darl named the girls. "Whooee, that's Sissy. Yessir."

I gagged, stuffing my forearm against my mouth to keep the sound from reaching the men near the trailer. The men the Devil occupied clear through to their souls.

Fighting down tears, I wondered how the evil of these men could be allowed to exist.

Meanwhile, Chet and Ernie thought Bud's claims of infamy to be awfully funny. Hearing them laugh made my stomach roil.

Chet's drawl overtook the vile laughter. "Bud, all kidding aside, Greg, Ernie, and me owe you some real thanks for making introductions, so to speak. Leading the way and all that. If you hadn't told us how you did it, I don't know that we would've done more than think about how pretty all the young girls are around here. God's flock sure does provide, as you've said."

I heard the clap of a hand on a back, then the voice of Greg, the new pastor of Little Clementine. "Following in your footsteps is a damn pleasure, Dad. You're an inspiration. And we all came out on top, the way I see it."

Bud Darl laughed. "On top, in more ways than one. You boys better keep getting these photographs. You owe me that much. Just keep bringing me those pictures, and we'll stay on top of this town."

I gulped down air and tears, barely able to keep listening. They'd kill me if I confronted them. Me against four "pillars of the community?"

Any one of them would pick me up and throw me against the trailer in a second if I tried anything.

Instead, I dug my hands into the dirt, letting the blood from my nails soak into the ground.

Shaking, I crab-walked back along the side of the trailer, making strange noises, as I couldn't hold in my sobs any longer. The men were having too much fun to notice the sound of my escape, though.

Bud Darl crowed into the night. "Boys, this town is mine!"

I ran as my gut roiled with guilt at the knowledge that I'd never be brave enough to tell anyone.

That night, shocked as I'd been to hear them so brazenly and pridefully boasting of their sins, I'd only been able to freeze in horror and listen. Acting on the feeling in my stomach would have seen me vomiting as soon as I'd set eyes on them. As it was, I nearly got sick when I finally did make it home and locked the door tight behind me.

Tonight was different.

Mark 7:21 and 23 came to mind. "'For from within, out of the heart of men, proceed evil thoughts, adulteries, fornications, murders…All these evil things come from within, and defile the man.'"

I whispered the words, but they gave me the Lord's own strength. The memory of that evil night lived in me for a reason—to aid me in delivering God's plan.

Bud was evil. Sick and soulless and too old to participate in his former depravities, he'd still done what he could to set the Devil loose in other despicable men.

"You boys better keep getting these photographs. You owe me that much."

I'd found some of those Polaroids in Chet's house. I'd seen his hiding place, right there in Ellie Sue's room. A screw on the floor, right off the grate—so careless, so arrogant. Didn't take much to undo the rest, as they were all loose. And Rosemary allowing it. She had to have known. Why was this behavior allowed?

I could've stopped it, couldn't I? Spoken up, let someone else know. Someone outside of town.

That thought had wormed its way through my mind more than once over the years. And each time it'd come, I'd ignored it for the lie that it was. No one would listen to me, not in this town. And nobody from the outside could be trusted enough to do the right thing either. The sheriff was good for handing out speeding tickets to people passing through and damn little else.

No more.

The evil being done in Little Clementine could not be solved with words—not from me or anyone else.

Tonight, I'd brought more than words to Bud Darl's trailer. For I would lose nothing more to this town and its evil men. They had taken all they would from me.

I stepped out of the oak's shadow.

Even the mountain cold couldn't touch the heat of God's

grace driving me. Through the window, I glimpsed Bud by the light of his open refrigerator door.

My lip curled, disgust filling my heart over what had already been allowed to happen. Maybe in the very den I peered into now.

With Bud's limp, decaying body set upon by illness, he hadn't raped any young girl in years. Though he'd lived vicariously through his son and Chet and Ernie. He'd also been allowed to live for far too long without facing a single consequence.

Two down. Two to go.

I hefted my axe beside me, savoring the weight. The balance. I'd cleaned it since the last bloodletting, as befitted an instrument of God.

Now the weapon was ready for the next step on the Lord's path.

"Romans 3:21-23, 'But now the righteousness of God without the law is manifested, being witnessed by the law and the prophets; Even the righteousness of God which is by faith of Jesus Christ unto all and upon all them that believe; for there is no difference: For all have sinned, and come short of the glory of God.'"

The words filled me with fire.

With my hand on the doorknob grounding me in cold reality, I finally allowed myself to smile.

Tonight, the Lord's will be done.

23

Bud couldn't sleep. Instead, he stared blankly into the refrigerator.

Seventy-nine years old, and all he had to show for all that time was raging indigestion and the bladder control of a puppy. Useless organ at this point.

Would a few sips of buttermilk help, or just make things worse?

Making his decision, Bud pulled the buttermilk out and slammed the refrigerator door shut. He stretched up to the cupboards above the sink for one of his old bourbon glasses. He'd pretend the buttermilk was liquor, since his gut could no longer handle the good stuff.

Damn age.

Worse than his useless body, though, was the lack of respect he now had around town—what had once been his town. All the parishioners—*his* parishioners—listened to Gregory preach like the man was a damn archangel. None of Little Clementine's folks had ever gazed at Bud like that, all starry-eyed and worshipful.

No, but Gregory needed to be careful. Becoming an idol for these people wasn't healthy. "God will strike him down in a heartbeat if he gets too big for his britches. Too much pride'll bring a man lower than he could ever dream possible."

His grandson, Ian, was worlds worse than his son.

Ian was too soft by far, despite all Bud had done to toughen him up as a kid. He was a sissy who didn't deserve to be playing that organ every Sunday.

But I'm not the one making decisions any longer, am I? That's Gregory.

Taking his glass to his recliner, Bud settled back with a groan and nearly spilled his buttermilk as he lifted it to his lips. That was the way of things at his age.

He ran his tongue over his teeth, taking another sip. The drink's sourness matched his mood. "I know I'm too old. No question. I heard that man in town call me senile last week, don't think I didn't."

Unfortunately, age hadn't changed his views on his gutless family.

Gregory should have raised Ian better. Even ten years ago, Bud would've beaten the fear of God into that idiot boy. But Bud had made the mistake of leaving the chore to his son, whose head was bigger than his understanding of duty. Ian was running away from his duty like the pansy-ass mama's boy he was.

A picture of Bud giving his first sermon hung above the television. Head full of hair, mouth full of fire, body full of grit and determination and faith. Strong.

In my glory days, I was something.

He'd been a king back then, not so long ago in the scheme of things. A prince of God. To think of the adoration he'd garnered…

And then, boy oh boy, there'd been the conquests. He'd touched miles of taut, young skin, tangled his fingers in masses of soft hair, and tasted bubble gum in so many mouths. To think of the tiny gasps of his many virgin conquests and the way they'd bowed to his desires…

The holy spoils of his reign had been great.

Bud's memories were legion. He treasured every single one over and above the pictures other men of his congregation had gifted him over the years.

Bud Darl had broken in an entire generation of women. Blessed this town with his seed like no other man.

Oh, what I'd do to get a hard-on just one more time. I'd sell my soul.

An image of beautiful little Maybelle Sweeney and her sister, April, came to mind on that wish. Both of them with their pretty blond hair and their emerald-green eyes. The pictures he'd seen didn't do the girls justice, damn them. And neither girl would ever understand what she'd missed out on by being born so late…the pleasure of his flesh against hers in the dead of night, celebrating his wisdom and her innocence together. So young and smooth…

The front door to his trailer squeaked. Open and shut, like a thousand times before. Bud couldn't rise to action as he once could, but he managed to push himself up from his chair to at least face the direction of the door, half hoping the Sweeney girls had heard his prayer.

But no.

The person he'd always suspected would come for him eventually was standing there. It seemed that patience, while a virtue, had its limits.

Bud grinned, nearly giggling at the absurdity.

"An axe?" Bud laughed, actually laughed. "What do you think you're going to do with that? Copycat someone with some real balls?"

Last Vendetta

In his time, Bud Darl had been called many things. *Idiot* was not one of them. He knew, as the FBI agents said, Chet and Ernie's killer was probably among the Little Clementine populace. Bud knew hate often grew out of love. He, himself, with a self-aggrandizing son and a useless grandson, felt contempt for those closest to him.

Still, he hadn't quite expected this one. He was half impressed.

"You expect me to think you're the killer?" Bud stepped closer.

Silence was the only response.

"I know you heard us talking. More than once. I bet it's been eating you up inside, huh? But...you. You heard, you knew, and you did nothing. You know your place. Listen to your instinct now. That's God. He's telling you to go on home."

Bud sat back down, feeling every year of his age creaking in his old bones and joints. His backside settled against the chair seat, and he chuckled.

"Go on home, I said. You ain't gonna do a thing with that axe. Ain't got it in you." He gave a little flick of his fingers, as if to shoo away a fly.

The axe swung up, brushing the carpet...

"Bud Darl, you will answer for your sins."

Rage bubbled in Bud's throat, heartburn pounding up into his chest as a coconspirator.

This damn weak body, useless for any fight.

Bud felt the old spirit straighten his spine, urging him to almost stand. His voice, supported by the heated billows of his lungs, came out with all the fire and brimstone of his early preaching days. "I ain't got nothing to answer for, you stupid—"

The axe stole his righteous words away, meeting his neck below his ragged white hair and cutting into the paper-thin skin like a knife through butter. A sense of morality as sharp as the blade gripped, clinging to the edge of his consciousness, silent to the end.

His strength ebbed, buckling his legs, and he fell into the embrace of his old chair, his final throne.

24

Three o'clock in the morning didn't feel like a real hour of the day. Darkness settled over everything, reducing the world to the gleam of headlights. All three FBI Expeditions were parked before Bud Darl's trailer, their headlights creating a small bubble of light around the area.

In the white light of the SUVs outside, crime-scene techs waited for them to complete their walk-through.

Hesitantly, Emma took the point position and led the way into the trailer, only to be greeted with more blood and guts than she'd viewed in the last twenty-four hours.

Yet there was little enough of Bud Darl to view.

He'd been hacked into pieces that had, themselves, been hacked into pieces.

"That's a lot of hate."

Emma stood to the side of the doorway, her Tyvek suit rustling as she made space for Denae to step in beside her. They scanned the little trailer kitchen. The whole place was essentially painted in blood, so that the two agents had to work gingerly around the puddles of red, taking in the damage.

As the sheriff had reported on their arrival, Pastor Gregory Darl had awakened in the dead of night with the strong sensation that something was amiss, the light from his father's trailer shining into his and Julianna's bedroom.

Bud Darl never left the lights on. According to Gregory, he got beaten as a child if he left the lights burning.

Knowing that, the pastor left Julianna sleeping and went to investigate. He told the sheriff he passed Ian where he slept on the couch and walked out to his dad's trailer.

Making his way across the open dirt between their home and his father's, Gregory expected the man to be injured and stuck on the floor or, God forbid, unconscious from being struck down by a stroke. Instead, he'd found his father's remains all over the place.

Kneeling near one of Bud's almost detached hands, Denae cut Emma a quick glance. "Blood Darl sure left a mess."

Emma fought down a totally inappropriate chuckle. "Not that it doesn't fit, but did you mean to say *Blood* Darl?"

Denae blinked at her through curls that had fallen into her face. "You know what? I don't even know. I'm too tired."

Sheriff Lowell coughed from the doorway, standing in the bit of entryway that wasn't spattered with the ex-pastor's remains. Blood, bone, and gore were everywhere, and the sheriff kept his eyes on the agents, as if to ignore the macabre interior.

Unlike earlier, his face was pale, his hair stringy with sweat. Like he'd been trodden into the mud and trampled by a horse for fun. It appeared as if he'd aged a year since she'd last seen him yesterday.

"I'd hoped the murders were over. But this…this…"

Emma understood what the sheriff was getting at. "This is beyond brutal and reeks of a rage that surpasses the other murders."

The sheriff nodded. "I'll be outside if y'all need me. Just

wanted to let you know we've got everything taped off. I have deputies searching the surrounding property for any signs of the killer. You'd think we'd find some prints, but the ground is pretty solid this time of year."

Denae sighed. "Good luck. Murderer hasn't left footprints yet. Somehow."

Emma adjusted her stance as the hairs on the nape of her neck rose. The urge to follow the sheriff outside—maybe while screaming or begging him to call some other team of FBI agents to deal with this particular scene—gagged her with its intensity. Her bones practically trembled as she focused inward...because her physical reaction wasn't imagined.

This place was bad.

She waited for the sheriff to leave before she voiced her discomfort to Denae. "You can feel it, right?" Emma gestured around the room. "The hate? The fury in the air?"

Denae pushed curls back from her face and shook her head. She adjusted her gloves over her Tyvek sleeve, even though she hadn't touched a single item in the room. "I assume the question is figurative, in which case I agree. Absolute hate went into this murder."

Emma bit her lower lip while Denae walked toward the hall.

The problem sitting heavy in Emma's gut was that she'd meant the question literally.

It felt like she was breathing ice. Her lungs burned with the cold. The atmosphere of the trailer all but trembled with a rage she'd never encountered before. Anger—someone else's anger—thrummed like a low vibration against her spine, a veritable force of hatred demanding she leave and never come back.

And then she saw him.

Bud Darl sat in his raggedy reclining chair, in the far

corner of the little living room. He smiled a demon's grin at her. White, blank eyes stared from his jigsaw-puzzle face. Blood and muscle peeked through the cracks of his skin. His arms hung from his t-shirt sleeves with no more life than the pieced-together legs stretching from his decrepit boxer shorts.

The ghost's entire body was covered from head to toe in a deep-vermillion gore, with only rare bits of pale skin shining through. And his white-eyed gaze scorched Emma.

"I knew you were a devil woman. I'm surrounded by devil women." He lifted an arm, his hand dangling but his fingers still responding to his commands. His index finger pointed at her somehow. "You're a damn witch. Hand to God, I knew it. Why else would I be stuck in this place of purgatory instead of where I belong, with my Lord in His Heaven? You've laid a foulness upon me. Admit it!"

Emma detested this man, dead or not, but this was an opportunity she couldn't pass up. Bud wasn't the first ghost to appear to her in Little Clementine, but he was the first who'd spoken. If listening to him would stop the savagery unfolding in the town, she had no choice.

Picking her way along the blood-soaked carpet, aiming her plastic-covered boots at dryish patches, she walked deeper into the living area.

Checking over her shoulder to make sure none of her colleagues had followed, she turned most of her focus to the white-eyed ex-pastor and kept her voice low. "Tell me who did this to you, Mr. Darl. Tell me who the killer is so we can stop this."

Though an unearthly grin split his bloodied lips apart, he kept silent. Some of his teeth were black, offering the only relief to the red.

"Did you know about Chet? Ernie? Did you know what they were?" Emma stopped, staring at the grinning ghost who remained maddeningly silent. She had no problem believing he'd been a role model in evil, having seen his earlier behavior...and now this. "Were you sick like them? Molesting little girls? Protecting Chet and Ernie, maybe, as a leader in this town? Is that why you were murdered too?"

Bud closed his iris-less eyes and chuckled, blood slithering from between his lips. One of his ears dangled by a thread of skin and muscle and jiggled with the motion of his laughter. When he opened his mouth, his voice turned vile. "I'm not telling you anything, you devil witch. You got bigger problems than this mess, you surely do. I shouldn't even be talking to you, but I just couldn't pass up a chance to tell you something."

"Wha..." Emma swallowed, her words dying in her dried-up throat. Her body burned, even in the chill seeping into the little trailer every time the door opened.

"You have worse than this in your future." He leaned forward, his head wobbling before settling back on his neck. "Devil women can all rot in Hell."

The old ghost laughed again, blood squirting from his seams, his body barely holding itself together. The pitch of his mirth grew higher and higher until...he disappeared.

It was all Emma could do to keep her eyes on the floor and avoid stepping in pools of gore as she pivoted and hurried from the trailer.

She stumbled down the front stairs and rushed to the looming, bare-branched old oak. The tree was the stuff of nightmares. Long, empty boughs creaked in the chilly night breeze, sounding as if they would collapse on top of her.

Emma clutched her knees and sucked cold night air into her lungs, attempting to slow her breathing.

From the corners of her eyes, she watched Leo step away from giving directions to Sheriff Lowell's forensic team. Though his footsteps drew nearer, she didn't raise her face to meet his gaze. She was too focused on telling herself that she was alive—she wasn't drowning in Bud Darl's blinding, icy hatred.

"You okay?" Leo came within a foot of her, resting one hand gently on her shoulder. Emma got a peek of mismatched socks above his black shoes. Probably he'd gotten dressed in the dark. "You shot out of there about as fast as you drive."

She fought the urge to scream—her throat incapable of forming words—and wished she could tell Leo that Bud Darl was inside, laughing in his recliner. More than anything, she wanted to tell him that Bud said she had "worse than this" in her future. So no, she wasn't super okay right now. She really, really fucking wasn't.

Instead, she inhaled and anchored one gloved hand on the towering oak. "I'm okay. Just…the smell of old Bud Darl and a lack of sleep got to me. Should've headed out of there sooner, when I felt the nausea coming on. Instead, I went deeper into the trailer." She looked up at him in an effort to drive the lie home.

Leo squinted as if he didn't believe her, but he finally nodded. He patted her shoulder once more. "Take a break. I'm gonna check in with Jacinda and see if she's got an action plan."

Emma stood straighter, relaxed her shoulders, and watched Leo head off toward the main Darl house, a dozen or so yards from their now-deceased patriarch's trailer. Ian's dwelling, which he would apparently soon abandon, stood quietly some distance away, across the empty dirt that served as a parking area for the family's vehicles. The Bureau SUVs occupied much of that space now, beside the pastor's luxury sedan and a smaller hatchback that looked as though it hadn't been driven in years.

As Leo disappeared into the family's home, Emma turned

back to the door of Bud Darl's trailer, thinking she should go back inside and continue examining the scene. As she approached, the heavy cold that hung about the place shocked her. It was deeper and more frigid than the night air could possibly be, even at this time of year.

Emma took a step back and immediately felt warmed again, having moved back from either the memory or the lingering presence of Bud Darl's ghost.

Exactly how many yoga classes does it take to handle this kind of friggin' nightmare?

25

Leo stood beside Jacinda in the loose circle of their team. They gathered at the head of the Darl family's driveway after more than five hours of guiding the forensic team on evidence collection. The process was tedious, but Leo didn't blame the inexperienced crime-scene techs.

The sheriff's office only maintained two full-time technicians, who also served as deputies. A third had been brought in from a neighboring county. None of them had seen anything close to what they encountered in the elder Darl's trailer.

To their credit, the forensic team did a more thorough job than had been done with the previous murder scenes. They'd managed to pull every blood-spattered piece of material, dusted every surface for prints, and painstakingly collected trace evidence. After this experience, those techs would be capable of working in the biggest cities with no problem. If they managed not to fall asleep on their feet.

Leo shook himself and slapped some warmth and wakefulness into his cheeks.

The sun tried to peep beyond the clouds, but it wasn't very successful.

Maybe we're lucky the dang sun doesn't feel like shining through the clouds today. Two birds with one stone...obscure the brightness of the blood and keep us cold enough to stay awake.

Jacinda stretched her back, and a couple of vertebrae popped. "After a thorough search, we found another stack of Polaroids in his bedroom closet. Older shots by the look of it. But the victims were still very young."

The search had, indeed, been thorough. The carpet was gone. Half the walls were gone. Bud's recliner had been carted off in a small moving van the forensic team had brought.

Everyone remained silent, palpable frustration flattening their expressions.

Leo scrubbed one hand through his hair and stated the problem out loud, mostly to keep his brain awake. "So our theory about the murders being some type of retaliation for sexual abuse might be on the money."

Vance grunted, scuffing one already-ruined shoe in the mud. "It fits for Chet and Bud here, but if we can't find evidence connecting Ernie to the molestation racket, there might be another motive still in play."

"Which is why we all need to keep our eyes and minds wide open." Jacinda clapped her hands together, rubbing them against the cold. "I need everyone on their A game. Do what you have to in order to stay awake and aware. The murder is fresh, and the victim was a former patriarch. Emotions will be at their peak. Emotionally distraught people spill information they otherwise wouldn't. I want us to hear what this community has to say. Understood?"

Everyone in the circle nodded.

Jacinda assigned teams to conduct interviews with those closest to Bud. "Both family, that being Gregory, Julianna, and Ian, as well as neighbors such as the Hardys, whose home is just down the road. Leo and Emma, please take the immediate family."

Leo led the way back down the driveway, ignoring the two deputies joking around near the street at the end of the drive. Even as grisly as this killing had been, no love was lost between the sheriff's department and Little Clementine.

"I think we should question husband and wife separately." Emma paused halfway down the walk to Gregory Darl's. "How about I pair up with Julianna while you talk to the good pastor?"

Anything that'll get us out of here faster.

"Makes sense to me."

Leo didn't have to knock when he reached the pastor's modest house. The pastor had seen them coming up the walk —he'd probably been looking out the very window that had a clear shot of his father's trailer. For once in the man's life, he didn't seem inclined to argue.

Gray-faced and stooped, wearing a faded green turtleneck, he seemed a different man from the one they'd encountered yesterday. His blue eyes were bright and red-rimmed, suggesting he must have been crying for some time. With having lost his father, it seemed his brimstone stubbornness had all but deserted him.

Leo offered what he hoped was a comforting, sympathetic expression. The man almost seemed to need a shoulder to cry on. *And who could blame him?* "Can you and I speak privately while Agent Last speaks to your wife?"

Gregory rubbed a hand over his brow and gave a slight groan. "I suppose so. What help I can offer, the Lord only knows. I...I don't feel quite myself, I'm afraid."

"That's more than understandable, Pastor Darl, and I'm sorry to intrude upon your grieving this way. If we can just get the details, as much as you can give us..."

The pastor swallowed and turned away, silent. He waved limply for Leo to follow him inside. For the first time since arriving in Little Clementine, Leo actually felt sorry for the man.

He exchanged a glance with Emma before following the pastor into the kitchen to sit.

His partner's eyes were a tad wider than normal, which told him she was as surprised as anyone.

"You know what happened." Gregory leaned his elbows and arms on the table, face turned down toward the wood surface. He gave a sudden heave, as if he might vomit, prompting Leo to search for the kitchen wastebasket. The pastor composed himself, wiping a hand across his mouth and looking Leo in the face.

Gregory's eyes weren't just red from crying or shock. Something else had ahold of the man.

"Mr. Darl, are you feeling ill?"

He nodded, wiped a hand over his brow again, and straightened in his seat, as if forcing himself to appear strong and steady. "I had a sip of moonshine last night before bed. Perhaps more than a sip, given how I'm feeling now."

"You drank unregulated distilled spirits. Is that normal for a town like Little Clementine?"

"We all have our means of coping, and we make our penance before God, as He calls us to do."

Leo noted the information before getting back to the interview.

"Were you alone last night when you were 'coping' with moonshine?"

The pastor stared at him for a moment. "We all had some. Myself, Julianna, and Ian. The strain of what our town has been put through has taken such a toll on me. On all of us. Was this your reason for speaking with me privately, so you could ascertain the legitimacy of my behavior, as if you were better suited than the Lord to pass judgment upon me?"

Leo redirected the conversation to avoid the pastor's volcanic tendencies gaining voice. "Mr. Darl, what can you tell me about...what happened last night, after you shared a nightcap with your family?"

Gregory grunted, but Leo couldn't tell if it was approval or derision directed at his choice of words.

"I told Sheriff Lowell what I saw. I don't know what more I can tell you."

"Just start at the beginning."

After a pause, the man did just that, telling the same story the sheriff had related a little after three that morning. Pastor Darl's voice broke off with emotion as he reached the point where the sheriff arrived. He cradled his head in his hands, massaging his scalp. Leo gave him the time and space to gather himself.

This was where they might get something—anything—that could help.

When the pastor spoke again, he was filled with self-blame. "I heard nothing. I don't understand how I could have heard nothing. We...my wife and son...spent the evening praying and discussing the prayer vigil, and yes, we had something to drink. The conversation dragged on, and I grew sleepy, so I headed to bed while Julianna cleaned and prepped for tomorrow. Ian said he would stay up to write some music."

"But you woke up at around three in the morning. Is that right?"

Gregory nodded, wiping a hand down his face. "Something woke me. It must have been the Lord calling me to attend to my father's passing. If only I'd awoken sooner. As soon as I turned over and saw that light...I knew something was wrong. Father lived so close. I should have heard the killer. It should have woken me. The trailer is barely a hundred feet away from the house."

This man is utterly broken. The murders are finally personal.

Of course, Leo wouldn't say that. "There was no sign of forced entry or even a fight, so it's not a surprise you heard nothing. It's not your fault. And, if you'd interfered, we may have had two Darl men murdered."

Gregory Darl shook his head, denying that he could be let off the hook that easily. "My father always refused to lock his front door. Made me nervous, but our community is so small. His stance was that someone who trespassed in his house…or ours, for that matter…was trespassing in the Lord's house, and they would pay the due consequences."

The man's voice strengthened ever so slightly. His arms tensed where they lay across the table as he raised himself up. By the time his eyes met Leo's, his hands were trembling. Not only was the man in mourning—he was scared.

"But my father was wrong. God didn't protect him. My father was chopped to…to bits…on his own blessed floor." He clenched his eyes shut, tilting his head toward the ceiling and rocking for a few seconds, as if seeking some new revelation from God. "I don't know, Agent Ambrose. I don't know. Maybe my father was out of favor with God. That's all I can think of."

"Any idea why he would have fallen out of favor with God?"

With Bud Darl involved in sexual abuse of minors, Gregory would possibly be the best witness. Bud had raised him, after all.

Slowly, the man opened his eyes and seemed to regain a bit of his former conviction, even as Leo studied him.

He seemed shaken to his core with grief and guilt.

"Mr. Darl…" Leo prodded as the silence stretched out. "Can—"

"*Pastor* Darl, please." The man sighed, and it sounded as if it came from his soul. "That's about all I've got left."

Station in his church treasured above all else. Noted.

Leo hid his sudden annoyance and kept going. "Pastor Darl, what kind of relationship did you have with your father when you were growing up? When your father was the pastor of Jubilant Ridge, I mean."

Stiffening, Gregory Darl sat up straighter and placed his hands in his lap, as if Leo would smack his hands with a ruler if he slouched. "My father wasn't a wishy-washy man. My mother died in childbirth, and my father didn't falter. He raised me with a strong hand, as befitted an upstanding man of faith."

Leo noted how the pastor had returned to the party line. He hoped to prod him into real, human reaction, though. "And does that mean you were often reprimanded? Physically?"

He shrugged, dismissing the question. "Whatever whoopings I got as a youth were well deserved. In the city, things might've changed, but in an old-fashioned community like this, it's not considered out of place to spank a child who's in need of a lesson. I was better for the way my father raised me. He taught me my role, my responsibilities."

Leo leaned in, keeping his narrowed eyes on Gregory. "And you never resented your father's methods of discipline? Perhaps there were other things your father did that seemed…unforgivable?"

"My father was a good man. Passionate and intimidating to some—"

"We found pictures of young girls. Naked. In your father's home."

"How dare you—"

"He punished you. He punished others. Maybe your resented him."

Gregory's eyes went wider, his nostrils flaring. Some of his previous fire returned. "I see what you're thinking, but I didn't do this. I'm not capable of doing this. I am a man of God, Agent Ambrose. You'd better watch your step if you and your team have any idea of accusing a son of the Lord of murder! I am a chosen man. Chosen by God Himself to lead this congregation, and therefore I am not to be trifled with!"

Leo allowed the pastor to breathe in his fire and brimstone. Gave it a few seconds to burn itself out.

"With all due respect, Pastor Darl, so was your father."

26

Emma waited until Leo and Gregory Darl disappeared into the kitchen before meeting Julianna in the small formal living room by the entry.

Separate rooms were definitely the way to go. Gregory had seemed cowed by the night's events, but Emma wouldn't put it past him to erupt. She'd prefer Julianna not jump up to go running to his side.

Or turn to him for her every answer.

The pastor's wife settled on the edge of the couch by the window. Emma dragged an old rocker—very similar to the rockers in the church's creepy jailhouse nursery—a little closer.

Julianna's eyes were dry, even though her father-in-law had just been slaughtered in their backyard. Her calm demeanor stood in stark contrast with how she had backed away after Bud burst into the nursery above the church.

"I am so sorry for your loss, Mrs. Darl." Emma quieted her voice, playing the confidante. "I know it must be difficult for you to talk this soon. How are you handling this latest tragedy?"

Lips pursed, Julianna nodded, then spoke as if she were reading from a script. "It is awful, but the Lord knows every man's time. Nothing happens without His approval. Nothing."

But do you approve of someone hacking your father-in-law to bits, Mrs. Darl?

Emma let the silence settle between them, giving the woman space to talk. She wasn't disappointed.

Julianna adjusted herself on the couch, moving slowly, setting her hands down to steady herself before clasping them in her lap. "I believe it was the Lord's good grace that allowed us to sleep soundly, despite the horrible evil that took place. Though I don't know how Ian could possibly sleep on that couch."

Her father-in-law was taken apart like a mouse by a cat, and she's happy her family slept through it?

Maybe she knows who her father-in-law really was?

Emma chanced covering Julianna's clasped hands with hers. Julianna was holding back, and this was Emma's opportunity to dig up at least one of the town's secrets.

"What kind of relationship did you personally have with Bud Darl?"

Julianna's demeanor darkened. She opened her mouth to respond, closed it tight again, finally took a breath, and began to answer. "Bud was the pastor of our church since I was a small child." She squeezed her eyes shut, as if in pain, but her voice remained as flat as a balance beam. "My parents, God rest their souls, watched me as close as they could. I am thankful for their protectiveness."

Emma sat back in her rocker, giving Julianna physical space. She sensed what Julianna hinted at and didn't want to pressure a potential abuse victim. A sick feeling nestled in her stomach.

"Julianna." She breathed the woman's name as gently as

she could. "We found Polaroids of unclothed underage girls in Bud's trailer. Are you saying you're grateful that you were protected from Bud Darl specifically?"

Julianna's features hardened. She crossed one leg over the other, a classic defensive position. Her teeth gnawed at her lower lip. She glanced at the closed kitchen door. "You should speak to Lizbet Sweeney. Not me."

Emma waited for more, but Julianna Darl fell stubbornly silent this time. Finally, Emma prodded her again. "I should speak to Lizbet Sweeney specifically about Bud, you mean?"

Julianna tucked her hair behind her ears, even though there wasn't a hair out of place. "You know, I have some housework I really need to attend to. And I'd like to get to it so I can spend the day outside. I think it might still turn out to be a beautiful day."

She stood, leaving Emma sitting in the rocker. That pit of discomfort still curdled in Emma's stomach like bad cabbage.

"The Lord's sun is shining on us, after all, don't you think?" Julianna reached behind the couch, opening the curtains a touch wider. She offered Emma a warm, genuine —perhaps too-bright—smile before she left the room.

Emma remained frozen in the wooden rocker, pondering the end of their conversation and the woman's oddly serene disposition.

From behind the kitchen door, Pastor Darl thundered, "I am a man of God, Agent Ambrose. You'd better watch your step if you and your team have any idea of accusing a son of the Lord of murder. I am a chosen man. Chosen by God Himself to lead this congregation, and therefore I am not to be trifled with!"

Sounds like Leo's done too.

27

After getting bellowed at by the good pastor, Leo and Emma crossed the backyard to Ian Darl's three-room house on the edge of the property. Ian, looking almost as tired as his father, invited them inside and led them to the kitchen. Cardboard boxes labeled *Living room*, *Kitchen*, and *Bedroom* were scattered, half packed, in the living area.

Leo sat at the wooden table and angled himself away from a wall filled with feel-good Bible verses. If he hadn't already known this was the kitchen of the son of a preacher, the quotes would've given it away. Otherwise, the kitchen was wood paneled and unremarkable. The room was well kept, with the air of a space built for necessity rather than luxury.

Ian stood awkwardly in the kitchen, watching Leo and Emma get settled at his table. His eyes had the same redness as his father's, his brow the same furrows of confusion or exhaustion.

"Sandwiches? I'm afraid that's all I can offer for breakfast on such short notice. And most of my cookware has already been packed."

"No, thank you."

Ian turned away, putting a hand on the kitchen counter to steady himself as he opened the fridge. He pulled out a plastic container, a loaf of bread, and some condiments. As if that simple task had exhausted him completely, Ian put both hands out to support himself, drawing deep breaths before busying himself with the items he'd set out.

Emma cleared her throat, trying to grab Ian's attention. Leo added his own cough to the effort, but to no avail. The pastor's son didn't look around, and she shrugged before beginning their interview.

"This must be even more difficult for you, being so close to your grandfather's trailer."

His back to them, Ian gave a slight shrug. "I've been blessed to live my life so close to my family. This tragedy is a sign that the Lord's work happens where it happens."

Leo literally had to bite his tongue.

Close is right. Your little house is in your parents' backyard, not more than fifty feet from your grandfather's crime scene.

Ian placed a sandwich on a plate and began making another. His movements weren't shaky or nervous but definitely revealed a deep fatigue. That could have been grief working on him, or, Leo considered, it could be guilt.

"Do you feel that your grandfather's death is the Lord's work?"

Ian paused, setting the knife and mustard down and placing his palms flat on the countertop. "Death is always the Lord's work, regardless of the cause. If it had been a heart attack that took him, it still would've happened with my grandfather living nearby, I still wouldn't have known the moment he passed, and it would still be the Lord's work."

Finally finding his patience, Leo managed to get a few diplomatic words onto his sore tongue. "That's…very pragmatic."

Leo cut his eyes to Emma. From her expression, he got the sense that she thought Ian's reaction was strange too. She shrugged, as if to indicate that maybe he'd have better luck.

They'd refused sandwiches, but Ian remained focused on the task of making them. Egg salad, of all things. Not exactly what Leo would have ordered on a cold winter's day begun with blood and guts.

"I suppose you agents must travel away from your homes? Your religious communities too?"

"We do travel a fair bit." Leo pulled out his iPad, letting the device clank on the table to draw Ian Darl's focus.

He turned around to come to the table with a full platter of egg-salad sandwiches. Sitting down slowly and steadying himself against the table, he gestured to the platter and the water glasses in front of them.

"Help yourselves, please. God's work requires God's food. My mother made the egg salad." He blushed like a teenager, taking a sandwich for himself. "I'm a little embarrassed to confess my mother keeps my fridge stocked. It's a great blessing, though. I don't know what I'll eat in Baltimore."

"Mr. Darl—"

"Ian, please."

Leo cleared his throat to keep from shouting his frustration. He inhaled a deep breath. "Ian, are you also feeling the aftereffects of 'coping' with all that's been happening? Your father mentioned you and your parents enjoyed a little moonshine last night. It looks like you may have had a bit too much."

The blush returned. "Ah. Yes, my father speaks the truth. We did partake in spirits last night, all three of us. I'd intended to spend the evening writing, but I'm afraid you are correct in your estimation, Agent Ambrose. I was out like a light before I could put pen to paper."

"That's right. I forgot you write sermons." Ian had

supposedly been writing music, not a sermon, but Leo wanted to see how closely the family's stories lined up.

Ian took a delicate bite of his sandwich, then cautiously wiped his mouth with a napkin.

"My father allows me to give a sermon every so often, yes, but I was planning to work on my newest song. I like to combine my message with the original hymns I've composed. That keeps me busy." He grinned. "I'm no John Newton...from the looks on your faces, I see you're not familiar with the man. He wrote 'Amazing Grace.' Perhaps you've heard of it?"

Ian finished with a laugh but regained his composure when his eyes met Leo's, which Leo had kept as flat and emotionless as possible.

He held the man's gaze and continued their interrogation. "Your father mentioned you compose music. Did he expect you to follow in his footsteps?"

Emma's hunger, or perhaps her frustration, must have gotten the better of her in that moment, and she reached out and snagged half a sandwich.

Ian shifted his eyes to meet hers as he replied. "My father expects many things. I always seem to be a disappointment. I'm a Darl man by birth, but I am not cut from the same cloth as my grandfather or father."

Emma chewed for a moment. Leo was about to ask another question, but she swallowed quickly and picked up on Ian's comment. "Same cloth?"

"Yes. I only mean I have no...desire to lead the flock the way they have."

"Is that why you're moving to Baltimore?"

"As soon as I can."

Leo sat back in his chair, observing Emma and Ian as they broke bread together like old friends. Emma finished her sandwich first and washed it down with a swallow of water.

She stared hard at Ian, unblinking and focused...maybe thinking the same thing Leo was. Mild hangover notwithstanding, this guy was amazingly okay for someone whose grandfather had just been butchered within one hundred feet of where he'd slept.

Ian's father, Gregory, had been a mess, and Leo assumed Julianna Darl had been in a similar state—though he and Emma hadn't had much of a chance to talk yet. Their son seemed calm by comparison.

Tentatively, Leo sipped his water, waiting to see if they'd discover anything beyond humble pride coming from this man. Was Ian capable of murdering his own grandfather? What motive would he have?

He seemed wholly interested in his sandwich and not much else.

"It must be great to have such supportive parents." Emma offered a smile to the preacher's son. "Your mom makes a delicious egg salad."

"It's a blessing."

"You spent last night at your parents' house." Leo set a sandwich on the small tea plate in front of him, joining in the casual conversation.

Both Gregory and Julianna mentioned Ian had slept on their couch last night. If they'd both seen him there before and after the killing, he would have had an almost impossible time frame in which to sneak out, butcher his grandfather, return home, shower, and get back to sleep. All without waking his parents.

"Yes, I tend to, whenever we indulge as a family."

"How often does that happen?"

"Not very, if I'm being honest. We've all been a bit stressed, and spirits are the one indulgence the people of Little Clementine have allowed ourselves. I was so tired afterward, my mother just laid me on the couch. Father had already gone upstairs to bed by that point."

"Uh, Ian." Emma leaned forward, pulling his attention to her before he could focus on another sandwich. "If you don't mind my saying so, you seem awfully calm, considering what's happened. Are you going to miss your grandfather?"

The easy look dropped from Ian's face, and he straightened in his chair. His eyes darted to one of the biblical verses above Leo's shoulder, as if reminding himself of something the Lord had said.

"Of course. Absolutely." Ian frowned, sipping his water. "Bud Darl was a leader in this community."

"And was there anything he did during his life," Leo kept his voice even, unassuming, "which maybe fit into a different category? Something, uh, less than becoming of a man of God?"

"What do you mean?"

"We found photos, Ian. Pornographic photos of young girls and women in your grandfather's closet. Do you know anything about that? Heard any rumors?"

Ian's brow furrowed as he sat back in his chair, sandwich forgotten. "Whatever he did is between him and God now. I hope you understand that."

"I'm sorry." Leo sighed, hoping the apology sounded sincere. "But I had to ask. It's important to understand every aspect of a victim's life, the good and the bad."

Emma leaned forward. "These questions can be difficult, Ian, but you have to remember that asking uncomfortable questions is part of our job. Please don't take offense, okay?" She was playing nice, and Ian took the bait.

He nodded, wilting in his chair. "I'm being overly defensive." Ian swiped one hand through his reddish-brown hair. "I should be the one apologizing for snapping at you. Of course you must ask questions. I feel guilty, that's all, about sleeping on my parents' couch while my grandfather was…was…being slaughtered nearby. So close. I should've done something, but I didn't even wake up. How can someone sleep through something like that?"

Leo's throat stopped up with emotion. As a teenager, he'd slept on his grandparents' couch while his Papu had run out into the street. He'd been chasing Leo's own dog…and gotten hit by a car and killed.

The guilt he'd hung upon himself for that day's nap still weighed him down.

Therapists termed the complicated emotion *survivor's guilt*. There was nothing easy about living with the sense you should be dead in someone else's place, or that they'd died because of you.

Ian still had a long way to go before he'd feel true relief from that.

Emma coughed, her eyes on him instead of Ian. The memory must have shown in his face, but he shook himself and swallowed the lump in his throat. "Ian, try not to be too hard on yourself…"

Leo allowed himself to go numb as he spouted the same advice he'd never been able to listen to. The words came out feeling honest and sincere.

He'd practiced them often enough, to himself and others, that the lies came easily.

28

Cora and Bishop Hardy had mercy on Mia and Vance, providing them with fresh doughnuts and coffee powerful enough that Denae would've swooned. But a heavy pressure smothered the room. Tasty doughnuts and strong coffee aside, they were there because another murder had been committed, and it was worse than the previous four combined.

Compared to what Jacinda and Emma had described, the Hardys seemed far steadier than they'd been for their last interview. Perhaps not by much. At least their kitchen was warm and welcoming, which was more than could be said for the church or the community center.

"These doughnuts are delicious, Mrs. Hardy. Thank you." Mia held up the remaining little bits of her cinnamon selection.

The Hardys had insisted on serving refreshments before speaking about the case. After such a gruesome night, Mia had thought she'd never eat again. As soon as the doughnuts came out, however, she ate three in a row. She dusted the cinnamon off her hands, destroying the evidence of her weakness.

"Thank you for the food. It was a long night, as you can imagine." She gave the couple a grateful, dimpled smile. The dents in her cheeks endeared her to most people, convincing them to open up. "Perhaps we could get started?"

The couple nodded, and Bishop gestured for her to proceed. "Please do. My wife and I are prepared to assist you however we can, and may the Lord bless you all and aid you in your investigation."

Cora muttered a feeble, "Amen."

Mia waited for the moment to pass before asking her first question. "Do you know anyone who may have had a problem with Bud Darl?"

Bishop Hardy snorted, leaning back so far in the kitchen chair that it creaked. "Plenty of folks had a problem with Bud. That doesn't mean they had a problem with my Rosemary. Surely, all the deaths are connected?"

Vance leaned forward, saving Mia from the tirade. "We believe so, yes, but—"

"But nothing!" Bishop rose from the table and paced to the coffeepot, pouring himself a second cup. "Use your logic, man. Whoever killed the other four also killed Bud. Anyone could've had a problem with Ernie or Louise or even Chet. But unless we can point to someone who had a problem with or hated our Rosemary…"

The man's words became choked. He leaned over the countertop, facing away from them. At the table, Cora shook her head, breaking a doughnut apart into crumbs without lifting a single morsel to her lips.

"Sir, if we start with one person, we may find a connection between the entire group."

Mia's voice was gentle, but Bishop still whirled to face them.

His face was bright red. "More people than I can count had issues with Bud! He was going senile, is the truth of the matter, and riling up people every which way. But nobody quarreled with Chet as far as I know, and everyone loved our daughter."

"Not all feuds are public." Mia paused, considering her words.

At this point, it was possible Rosemary hadn't been aware of her husband's proclivities. And she might've been too scared to share the information with her parents, even if she knew.

Cora squirmed in her seat, brushing the mess of crumbs from her hands. Her coffee also sat untouched. Behind her, Bishop Hardy paced the kitchen like a caged cougar.

"Cora." Mia touched the woman's hand, aiming to transmit what calm she could. "Can you tell us what you know about Bud's relationship with the townspeople?"

The woman stared at the mess she'd created on the table. "Bishop is right. Plenty of people...even those who respected Bud when he was our pastor...have developed ill will toward the man over the years. For...for many reasons. Too many to make it worth your while to look into every one of them. But our Rosemary was just a child. Only twenty-six and sweet as sugar. Everyone loved her."

Vance stirred his coffee, not bothering to note anything on the iPad. So far, they had nothing new. "You say 'plenty of people' developed ill will toward Bud. Even if that's the case, some might've been more, ah, upset with him than others?"

Cora shoved to her feet, brushing down the skirt of her dress. She glanced at her husband.

With Cora's back to them, Mia couldn't decipher the wordless exchange.

She faced them again, straightening her back. "I need to check on the baby upstairs. But you should speak to Lizbet

Sweeney...er, Somerson now. Bo Somerson's wife. That's all I'll say on the matter."

Before Mia could respond, Cora hurried out of the kitchen. Within seconds, her feet thudded up the stairs.

Bishop Hardy didn't flee the room like his wife, but he appeared lost...bereft. Leaning back against the counter with his coffee cup tilting dangerously in his hand, he stared at the kitchen wall as if he'd understood nothing of the previous exchange.

Emma described him as a ghost. She was being kind.

"Sir, Mr. Hardy? Do you have anything to add?"

He gulped, his gaze remaining lost in the floral wallpaper above his kitchen table. Finally, he came back to himself enough to shake his head. "Cora's never told a lie, not on any day in her life. If she says to speak to Lizbet Somerson...then you had best speak with Lizbet Somerson."

29

Sitting in the front seat of the Expedition, Emma stuffed the last bite of a second egg salad sandwich into her mouth. She forced herself to chew and swallow. She hated egg salad. Always had and always would. At best, the stuff was salty and pickle-y and overly mushy. At worst, it was tasteless and made you feel like you'd coated your mouth with paste.

Beggars couldn't be choosers, though. Both Emma and Leo had decided they couldn't turn down free food at this point. Not when Ian Darl wrapped up a to-go bag over their protests. They'd had no other real prospects for breakfast. It had been a long morning.

"Edible enough." Leo pulled a napkin along his fingers. "Though I wish I'd kept some leftovers from last night instead."

"Would've stayed cold in here too." Emma turned up the Expedition's heater.

Their little section of roadway was currently deserted.

Leo's iPad sat on the dashboard. Jacinda would be calling them into a conference any minute.

"What'd you think of the good pastor's son?"

Emma thought about Ian Darl's flat reactions. "He seemed off, which is to be expected, right?"

"Right."

"But he seemed *off* off."

Before Leo could respond, his iPad dinged. "There's Jacinda." Leo settled the iPad more firmly between the two of them and swiped up the volume. "Right on time."

"Everyone hear me?" Jacinda sat at a table. Emma could just see the side of Denae's face to Jacinda's right and what Emma assumed was Sheriff Lowell's shoulder to Jacinda's left. Vance and Mia peered into their own cameras, appearing in separate little boxes on the iPad screen. Once everyone nodded, Jacinda continued. "All right, I have your shorthand notes, but let's hear it. Where are we? Emma and Leo, you're closest to the crime scene."

"Not much to report." Leo scratched his jaw. "None of the Darl family seemed willing to share anything about Bud other than him being an upstanding citizen. Though neither Julianna nor Ian seemed all that traumatized by Bud's loss. Gregory's pretty torn up. You all saw the beginning of that this morning."

That's my cue.

"Julianna did hint that Bud may have gotten what he deserved." Emma paused, letting the rest of her team absorb that tidbit. "She said we should speak to Lizbet Somerson, formerly Lizbet Sweeney."

Mia's eyes widened. "We got the same advice. Cora Hardy said the same thing, to speak to Lizbet."

Jacinda narrowed her eyes. "She say anything else, Mia? Vance?"

Vance shook his head. "Not really. Cora refused to give any specific information. Her husband only said a lot of people weren't fond of Bud."

"Sounds like the rest of the story is Lizbet's to tell." Emma's flat comment prompted nods.

Jacinda adjusted her screen and leaned back. "We tried checking in with the Somerson family again, but Lizbet wasn't home. Bo told us she often goes for walks when she's upset. He couldn't say for sure when she might be back, but he said she wouldn't miss the service tonight."

Emma and Leo started talking at the same time, but he held back, motioning for her to go first.

"Seems odd for a man in Little Clementine not to know exactly where his wife is at all times, doesn't it?"

"Emma took the words out of my mouth, Jacinda."

"That makes two of us, Leo. But I have the distinct feeling Bo isn't like the other men in Little Clementine. He doesn't seem to be one to follow the community leaders' examples too closely."

Mia's face filled the frame. "We have an upset female member of a community that keeps track of all its women. She's known for taking solitary walks with an undetermined time frame, and she's missing the morning after the former patriarch was murdered. Is anyone else thinking what I'm thinking?"

Jacinda was the first to respond while everyone else made mutterings of agreement in the background.

"Lizbet Somerson could be our perpetrator, yes. That's a possibility we have to consider. She could also be a woman grieving or, as her husband said, simply upset by what's been happening in this town. I don't know who wouldn't be upset by such devastating events."

Emma raised a hand, and the SSA nodded. "Are we going to look for her or wait for her to return? If she *is* our perpetrator, she could be fleeing right now. Bud Darl sort of feels like an ultimate act, because of his former station and the brutality of the murder. That was the definition of escalation."

"That's a good point, Emma. Bo assured me his wife would return from her walk at some point. Like all the community members, Lizbet is supposed to be at the evening service. So we talk to her there."

The matter didn't feel settled to Emma, but the SSA had already moved on.

"I'm afraid we got little else from the rest of the Somerson family." Jacinda scowled into the camera. "Bo's stepdaughters, the Sweeney girls, seemed shocked to hear about Bud's passing. But everyone in the family had alibis. Each other."

Of fucking course they did.

"That's the big issue in this town, right?" Emma leaned toward the iPad, not trying to keep her sarcasm in check. "Everyone here lives in such tight little boxes. There's always someone else to vouch for them. But just because you believe your loved ones are in your home doesn't mean they haven't run off somewhere without your knowledge."

"The alibis are flimsy at best." Leo sighed beside her. "Unless all those people were sitting around in a circle, staring at each other and holding hands."

Emma barked a humorless laugh. "Sounds like a hot Saturday night in this town."

Mia laughed as the others shook their heads, but nobody disagreed with Emma's comment.

They couldn't.

Jacinda waved for attention. "Look, what Denae and I found most troubling is the fact that Wade Somerson is nowhere to be found. Again. Bo said his dad's busy and probably off working a job."

"And it could be true." Denae's face shifted from side to side in the camera as she adjusted her seat.

Jacinda picked up the conversation. "It could be true, yes. And yet, we all know what it looks like."

"Exactly my thinking, Jacinda." Leo raised his voice, all but growling into the iPad. "I'd say it's been Wade this whole time. I wanted to search through his house again yesterday, but he was nowhere to be found. Wade may have slaughtered Bud Darl and jumped ship, and unlike Lizbet, he has a vehicle and has close to a twenty-four-hour head start."

Emma curbed the impulse to lay a hand on Leo's elbow and calm him down. This was only their second case together, but she'd seen his passion in action. It wasn't beneath Leo to chase Wade Somerson down. Even though, she suspected, his attitude was currently built on exhaustion as much as anything.

"But what's Wade's motive?" Emma leaned in toward the iPad, raising her voice over the sound of a car speeding by. "I can't help thinking, from the sound of it, plenty of people might have willingly killed Bud. Whoever murdered him may have done so because Bud was guilty of the exact same sins as Chet."

Leo wasn't done chewing that bone, though. "Or Wade's running because he's an amateur photographer who knows exactly who's in all those pictures we've found, because he's the one who was taking them."

Nobody had a reply to that.

Emma sat back in her seat, and silence ruled the vehicle for a moment.

Short of another ghost visiting her—which she'd just as soon avoid after the way Bud treated her—they had very little to go on.

Jacinda conferred with Sheriff Lowell slightly off-screen, then came back on camera. "Emma and Mia, you two should speak with Lizbet as soon as possible. If you run into her in town, fine. If not, then at tonight's evening service, assuming she appears. I think she might respond better to women. But we'll have two teams at the service, keeping an eye on the good people of Little Clementine. Mia and Emma, take the service itself. Vance and Leo, take the church perimeter. Sheriff Lowell will call with anything the M.E. has to add, but I'd say it's pretty likely this was another murder by the same perpetrator with the same axe. However, on the off chance we're wrong, Denae and I will staff the phone here in case anything gets called in."

"And in the meantime…?" Emma raised an eyebrow.

"In the meantime," Jacinda stretched and pushed herself back from the table, "everyone get back to the motel and take a damn nap. Briefing over."

Leo shut the iPad cover flap, grunting with satisfaction upon putting the device away.

Apparently, he was ready for a break too.

Emma refastened her seat belt and pulled out onto the highway.

The crick in her neck begged for a hot shower and a firm pillow. All of them certainly needed a break, in more than one manner of speaking. While Emma wasn't looking forward to the bed itself, she was thrilled about the sleep part of the equation.

Assuming the ghosts would allow it.

30

Later that afternoon, after a thorough power nap, Emma pulled up to the Jubilant Ridge House of Faith. It was forty minutes before the service, but the parking lot was already full. Beside her, Mia grunted in annoyance, which would've been funnier if Emma hadn't felt the same.

Emma opened her door and stepped out. "Never too early to start praying, I guess."

"Funny." Mia pointed to the marquee sign in front of them. "Pre-service prayer starting at five thirty. Because, of course, there's a pre-prayer prayer."

Emma set off at a fast walk, Mia trailing behind her. "That gives us a ten-minute window to find Lizbet and get her to talk before we have to cause a scene."

Inside, Emma came to a stop at the back of the church and digested the crowd.

Everywhere she looked, people were scattered among the pews with Bibles and hymnals in their hands. Some chatted quietly while others just read or waited.

The space felt closed in and dim. Electric lighting and

shiny wood beams did nothing to change Emma's claustrophobic perception.

Nearly the whole town was gathered. As she searched the pews, she noted Wade Somerson was, once again, MIA.

She and Mia still had ten minutes before they'd be forced to either wait or start a whole different kind of protest. Emma scanned the attendees, thankful for the first time that the town had so few citizens.

She laid eyes on Bo first, standing in the center aisle, speaking with two older men. She spotted his wife a second later, sitting on the edge of a pew near the stairway door, off to the left of the chapel. Emma caught Mia's attention. "There."

"Got her." Mia reached Lizbet first, with Emma right on her heels.

Lizbet sat alone, staring blankly down at her hymnal. Mia slipped into the pew and stole a seat beside her before the woman even realized they'd approached.

"Mrs. Somerson, do you remember me? Agent Logan." Mia gave her sweetest smile, full of dimples. "We're hoping we could ask you a few questions?"

Emma stepped up to the pew. "How about we go up to the nursery and sit down for a few minutes in private?"

Lizbet glanced between Emma and Mia, her mouth forming a horrified O. "You must be joking. The service is about to start. Agents—"

"Lizbet," Mia leaned closer, ever the confidante, "we understand you want to be here, but this is important. We're trying to avoid future memorial services."

The woman focused back on her hymnal. "Absolutely not. Perhaps afterward. I'm afraid I can't miss a minute of this service, not with all that's been happening. It'd be disrespectful."

Emma knelt, getting on Lizbet's level. The other agent's

polite approach was usually the better way to go, but courtesy wasn't going to work right now. They needed to talk to Lizbet Sweeney, whether she liked the timing of the conversation or not.

Secret-keeping time was over.

Leaning in, Emma placed one hand on the hymnal to block Lizbet from shutting them out by reading. "Lizbet, we can question you about your previous interactions with Bud Darl right here and now for the congregation to hear. But we'd really like to respect your privacy."

The woman jerked in her seat, as if it were charged by lightning. Stutters of protest worked themselves from her lips, and she glanced back at Mia, as if for aid.

The other agent's smile was pinched. "We need to talk to you," she said simply. "Where we do that is your only choice."

Lizbet shut her hymnal and took a deep breath. "The nursery, then. Lead the way."

Emma tried for a gentler smile now that the woman was cooperating. There was no need to terrify her.

But as she led the way up the stairs, Emma realized the woman didn't seem terrified at all.

Lizbet Sweeney wasn't worried about being arrested.

More like she's resigned. Like this is the end of a road she's been traveling.

What that resignation meant they'd soon find out.

In the dim little nursery, Emma pulled together three rockers and perched across from Lizbet. Mia settled down beside her and nodded to Emma. They resumed their roles from downstairs. Mia would play the friend, Emma the interrogator, and they'd hopefully get what they needed.

Emma braced her feet, trying to remain still and keep some professionalism for herself in the odd little space. "We've been trying to sort out reasons anyone in the community might've disliked Bud Darl. Cora Hardy directed us your way. Julianna Darl mentioned your name as well. You can see why we're so intent on talking to you as soon as possible."

Lizbet froze at the mention of Cora Hardy, then wilted upon hearing Julianna's name. She bit her lip. Both her hands gripped her knees...grounding herself. Tears welled in her eyes. Mia pulled forth some tissues.

"I've kept quiet for so long now." Lizbet sniffled, taking the tissues with a nod of thanks. "And nobody has ever asked. Not outright like this."

Mia muttered something under her breath—Emma thought it sounded like, *Of course not*. But then Mia offered a soft, encouraging smile. "I know it's hard, I promise I do. But you shouldn't have to carry whatever you're carrying. So we're asking now. Please help us. Tell us what happened."

The woman wiped her tears away, as if irritated they were present. "Bud...Bud raped me when I was a teenager. Many, many times. So many times, I couldn't give you a number if I tried."

The confirmation took Emma's breath away.

So many times, she's lost count.

The woman's pain echoed out from her every word.

Mia gripped Lizbet's hand in support. Her other hand white-knuckled the rocking chair arm, as if to gain strength from the solid wood.

Lizbet gave a dark little chuckle. "He thought nothing of it, or of any of us. He raped Grace Somerson too. Wade's wife. But Grace is gone, God bless her. She's safe from all the pain now. I guess it's left to me to tell her story, then, isn't it?"

Mia murmured comforting words.

Emma sat silent, wondering. Grace was gone. If Grace's ghost had been willing, she could come and tell her story to Emma anytime she wanted.

Which begged the question...how strong must the hatred

toward Emma be in the Other? Why else would Grace keep silent about something like this?

Her lips felt suddenly dry, parched. The atmosphere of empty cradles and church music rising up from below only made her nerves tingle more.

Emma leaned forward. "Can you tell us how he would do it?"

Lizbet took a deep breath, gathering herself. When she spoke again, her voice was robotic. "It always happened at celebrations where the adults were drinking. Easter, Christmas, the Fourth of July. Anytime the town gathered. Pastor Bud would give me punch. At first, I thought he was being kind, you know?"

Emma gave a small nod. "I know."

"But the drink was spiked, probably with the moonshine that Pastor Darl's family has always made. But I think there was something else. I was always so sleepy. I don't even remember everything. I know it happened, but I can only get bits and pieces of memory about it. And when I'd wake up, I'd be so stiff and sore, like I'd slept for a whole day. My head, and…everything just hurt." Lizbet clasped her hands protectively in her lap.

The picture became clearer for Emma. Bud—probably Chet and Ernie as well, maybe other men—would drug the girls' drinks or snacks and assault them. And her description of the aftereffects rang like a bell in Emma's mind.

"Lizbet, how many women in this community might have their own story to tell about Bud Darl?"

Rocking in her chair, Lizbet shook her head. "I couldn't possibly say. For the most part, we women have stayed quiet. No one would believe us over a pastor. My parents thought I was blessed to receive such personal attention. I have suspicions…I could write a list of likely victims for you, I guess, but there'd be no certainty in it.

And besides, I think it would just be the tip of the iceberg."

"What do you mean?" Emma needed Lizbet to be crystal clear, so she kept her voice gentle but firm. "I know this is hard, but I need you to be strong, please. Why would it be the tip of the iceberg?"

The woman sighed, using the last of Mia's tissues to wipe her eyes. The tears, which had leaked out as she spoke, stopped. She appeared years older and emptied out. Exhausted. The long-buried secret was out. Lizbet could see the other side of the crossroad now.

"Bud Darl has paid for his sins now…and maybe we should all just be satisfied with that." She gestured with the tissues still curled in her hand, gently disengaging her fingers from Mia's. "Thank you for the tissue. I hope I've helped. I really need to get to that prayer service now."

Emma didn't try to stop the woman as she hurried out of the room. Her words had been firm and set, making clear that she was done.

Meeting Mia's stare, Emma could only shake her head in temporary defeat. There were no good answers right now. Bud was a child rapist. A monster.

And so was Chet, most likely.

"Well, our suspect list just increased exponentially. Every woman in Little Clementine." Mia blew out a deep breath.

Emma took that moment to tell Mia about the Darl family drinking moonshine last night and how they all appeared to be hungover this morning.

"You think they were drugged? That would mean the murderer was drinking with them too."

"Or it was someone who knew about the moonshine and swapped bottles or added the drug without the Darls' knowledge. All three of them looked worse for the wear, including Julianna Darl."

"That doesn't mean we can scratch her name off our list."

"No, it doesn't. But we're probably better off looking elsewhere anyway. We have a definite motive for Bud. Probably for Chet and Ernie too, if they provided the drug or participated themselves. But if you're a woman out for revenge against a gang of rapists, why kill Louise and Rosemary?"

"They allowed it to happen? Or, at least, the killer thinks they did?"

Emma sighed. Part of her couldn't help but think—if their suspicions were true—this all had a grim sort of justice.

The problem was—whoever had hacked Bud and Chet and Ernie to pieces had also killed two women who, most likely, had been victimized by those men as well. These crimes should've been reported and dealt with by law enforcement. Vigilantes seldom kept justice in sight when vengeance was so satisfying, and that meant the killing might not be done.

Little Clementine was a damaged town. Emma felt it the first day they'd driven up. She thought they were a step closer to catching the killer. Undoing the pain that lingered behind closed doors in Little Clementine, though, under the protection of a church…there wasn't enough time or justice in the world to make that a possibility.

Not in this realm of reality anyway.

31

The broom closet's thin walls, next to the old nursery, hid none of Lizbet's words or the federal agents' conversation afterward. This had been a most productive little talk. The number of suspects had increased. The agents would be looking in so many directions that I had time to finish my mission.

Poor Lizbet Sweeney Somerson. The submissive, meek woman had deserved much better in her life. She hadn't earned what she endured from Bud or from her first husband, that wretch of a man. But Lizbet's new husband, Bo Somerson, was of a different stripe.

Bo was loving, but such a confused boy.

I listened as the agents' footsteps disappeared down the stairs. When all the creaks settled, I stepped out of the closet —much like Bo should've done years ago.

A small chuckle rattled my throat. "Leave it to Lizbet to marry a gay man."

The Somerson wedding had been the beginning of the end for me. A community event. Attended by the entire flock. Presided over by Pastor Gregory Darl, the ceremony had been filled with platitudes to cleave to each other, to honor and obey *'til death do you part.*

I felt pity for both Lizbet and Bo. The years stretched before them, filled with lies and secrets.

Speaking from experience, I knew that living lies and keeping secrets was no life at all.

"But go with God."

Ian had stood with Bo as his best man. More than once, Bo had cast small sideways glances his way. And I understood there were many, many secrets here in Little Clementine.

The music started downstairs, and I heard our pastor's voice calling the righteous to rejoice and make a joyful noise. Cries of glory mixed with pleas for salvation. But nowhere did I hear a single sound that resonated with honesty.

All of us were devout liars, unwilling to shatter our communal illusion with the truth. These secrets were coming out, though, oh yes. The Lord in His righteousness was shining light into the darkness.

And I, with my axe, was hacking holes in the wall to let the light shine through.

It was time to finish the final liars.

32

Fifteen minutes into the prayer service, Emma knew for certain she was in a different world.

Stationed in the back of the chapel beside Mia, Emma leaned against the back wall. She tried to will her body through the drywall and away from the spectacle before her.

Ian Darl began by belting out a lively, upbeat hymn.

From the sidelines, Pastor Gregory Darl encouraged his congregation to "dance the Devil away."

"Though our sorrow is great, we will not be held down by evil. We will dance!" The pastor's voice vibrated off the walls, driving the congregation from their pews into the surrounding aisles.

The few who remained in the pews stood and bobbed in place, clapping their hands out of time with the pastor's rhythm. One man swung his hands high in the air, giving Emma a sneer of derision. She and Mia were the only ones not dancing.

Mia nudged her shoulder. "Maybe we should clap?"

Discomfort swirling in her gut, Emma forced her hands

together. She and Mia were the only ones clapping on the downbeat...everyone else seemed to be half a step behind. But Emma soldiered on.

All around them, men, women, and children kicked and swung their bodies along with the upbeat music, sometimes bouncing into each other or the walls as they followed their pastor's rallying. The whole building shook with celebration.

Emma started experiencing motion sickness.

Then, with no warning, the music turned somber.

The FBI agents sent two loud claps through the dead-silent air.

Embarrassed to her core, Emma tucked her hands into her armpits. Mia shoved her hands into her pockets with equal speed.

"What the..." Emma's murmur was drowned out by the thumps of knees hitting the chapel floor. Parishioners fell into prayer, prostrating themselves. Their noses lowered to the ground, and their hands clasped before them where they knelt.

"Pray!" Pastor Darl lifted his hands to the ceiling, his eyes upraised. "Pray through the Holy Spirit. Pray, my friends. For all of us and the good of our community, we pray!"

A jumble of voices rose up. Emma couldn't decipher individual words, even from the men and women who knelt closest to her. Unidentifiable strings of sound bled from the lips of the congregation. The susurrations were so steady and hissing that Emma almost believed the people weren't even pausing to breathe.

She'd heard about this "speaking in tongues," sure, but she'd never witnessed it.

The cacophony grew louder. Emma pressed herself against the wall, as if she could shrink away from the otherworldly scene before her.

She glanced at Mia, who only shrugged. Her confused expression suggested this was a first for her too.

Mia's parents were Catholic, Emma remembered. Emma's own parents had been nonreligious—her father's passion for the law was probably the closest she came to religion.

Apparently, this was an experience neither of them would soon forget.

After nearly an hour of worship, yo-yoing between dancing, singing, and praying, Pastor Darl finally lifted his hands and called for his people to return to the pews for the sermon.

Emma barely kept from releasing a sarcastic laugh, managing to throttle the expression into an obnoxious, inappropriate sigh at the last moment.

More than an hour into the service, and they were just getting around to what she'd thought had been the whole purpose.

"Brothers and sisters." Pastor Darl gave an expansive wave of his hands. "Thank you for joining us in prayer to fight back the evil that has come upon us."

Emma scowled. "Looks like they can catch the bad guy without us."

Mia chuckled, barely loud enough to reach the other agent. "Hush. You want us chased out of here by an angry, grief-stricken, spellbound mob?"

Their voices were low enough that nobody heard the exchange.

Pastor Darl prattled on in blissful ignorance of Emma's skepticism.

"Today, we speak of the evil that lurks among the holiest of people, striking like a snake in the night. A snake, I tell you, that serves as an extended hand of the Devil, of whom we must all be aware…"

Emma listened intently, but the words offered no fantastic reveal. He spoke of his father's demise, as well as the other victims, praising their faith while decrying the evil that had stolen their lives.

He is a very good speaker. Charismatic.

When the sermon finally ended—more than an hour and a half after it had begun—Pastor Darl appeared to deflate. His voice grew hoarse over the course of the long-winded exploration of evil's invasion of the small community. He gave a hand gesture that communicated the congregation should kneel.

As one, the men and women in the pews went to their knees and bowed their heads.

"We will pray." The pastor knelt, too, on a cushioned stool beside the podium. "Remember First Corinthians 2:5, my friends, 'That your faith should not stand in the wisdom of men, but in the power of God.' Have faith in Him. Give the Lord your worries and let Him take the burden. We pray."

Emma caught Mia's eye and gestured toward the door, mouthing, *Go.*

The agent nodded.

As they made their way to the exit, soft sobs carried through the air along with murmured prayers. Many people were flat on the floor again. Some of them sobbing, some of them laughing, and several of them, once more, speaking in tongues.

Outside, Emma moved away from the entrance until she could no longer hear the emotional goings-on within.

The air was fresher outside, and the cold felt good.

Mia walked backward, keeping her eyes on the door, as if afraid they were being followed. "I've never seen anything quite like that."

Emma started to respond but stopped.

As weird as what they'd just witnessed might've seemed to Mia—and her—it wasn't any weirder than her new ability to see and speak to ghosts.

"Normal" was a relative term...now more than ever.

33

Vance's breath plumed into the night air. "I don't know what's going on inside that building, but I'm sure glad it's Mia and Emma in there instead of us."

"Amen, brother, amen." Leo paused. "Except I bet they're a lot warmer."

Leo had spent his youth in quiet churches. This one seemed to be vibrating with sound, but he had no desire to see the spectacle for himself. Whatever was happening—and whatever warmth might be offered—inside, he'd be content to get the report from his colleagues.

He rubbed his arms through his coat, trying to get some blood flow.

For now, he and Vance kept lookout from the relative distance of the trees lining the parking lot. Should anyone need help inside, they'd be ready.

And should anyone come outside to offer up secrets to the sky, they hopefully wouldn't notice the agents.

"I don't know if Jacinda and Denae got the short end of the stick or not." Vance shifted his stance, propping one boot against a tree trunk. "That community center is no less creepy than this churchyard."

"It's an even bet."

Jacinda and Denae had taken up their post at the community center, serving as a central base of command if something happened.

Personally, Leo would've preferred the community center to the encroaching woods and the vibrating church…but he could see Vance's point.

However, as far as he was concerned, the answers were inside this church.

Maybe we should've gone in with them. If something happens to Emma and Mia, we're not going to hear anything short of a gunshot with all the noise coming out of that place.

Leo was just about to suggest they at least go up to the entrance and peek inside when a side door swung open. Thanks to the lamps attached to the outside, he recognized April Sweeney erupting from the side of the building, followed by Maybelle.

Giggling, the sisters gripped each other's arms in camaraderie as they hustled toward a dilapidated swing set in the churchyard. Their breaths steamed up. The night air had to be below freezing, but the girls moved as if it were summertime.

Leo and Vance moved quietly, inching along the tree line until they were within hearing distance of the siblings. Between dusk and the foliage, they kept well hidden.

Thankfully, the girls were too intent on their own hushed gossip to notice.

"…never going to get Ian Darl to marry you," Maybelle was telling April as the two sat side by side on creaky swings, "if you keep ducking out of sermons! He's moving anyway."

"Ha! He hasn't left yet." April swung forward and back. The

chains on the swing must've been freezing, but she held on. "But I don't give a hoot about any of it. Not anymore. You hear Pastor Gregory in there? Talking about Bud and Chet and Ernie, saying all those nice things about them? It makes me sick!"

Leo glanced at Vance, who nodded to confirm he could hear the girls just fine.

This might be our lucky break.

Maybelle kicked her heels into the dirt beneath the swing set, pushing herself into a rhythm that mirrored her sister's. "I don't understand why you get so upset about what we did with Chet and Ernie. Hell, I kind of liked it. It felt good. Aren't you going to miss our special prayer sessions in the woods? Just a little?"

Swallowing down a curse, Leo shot Vance an uncomfortable frown. "And that just confirmed Ernie's involvement."

What the girls called "prayer sessions" the agents knew was rape.

These teenagers were naive enough, or possibly so brainwashed, that one of them giggled about it. How early had those men started grooming them?

"Well, won't you?" Maybelle prodded her sister when she didn't answer.

"I will not!" April hissed. "I didn't like it at all. Those grubby old men. It should make you sick too. Mark my words. The pastor's getting the axe next."

Maybelle giggled. "No way, Ms. Goody Two-Shoes. No one dares to touch Pastor Greg. I'm kind of bored without Chet and Ernie around, you want the truth." She swung harder, and Leo guessed the burst of movement helped her keep warm. "Those agents are awfully handsome, though."

Leo was so stunned he very nearly fell against the tree concealing him. Vance muttered something about needing to get the hell out of this town already. Leo couldn't have agreed more.

First things first, unfortunately.

"Maybelle, you're dumber than a chicken with its head cut off if you think those agents'll give you a second look."

On that note, April leapt off the swing at the apex of her upward lift. She landed on her feet and stumbled forward, then shot up, disappearing into the woods. Her swing clattered against Maybelle's.

Leo gestured after the girl who'd fled. "One of us should follow her."

"We should not be alone with these girls. I don't trust them." Vance grimaced at the thought.

"She has information on Chet Crawford and Ernie Murray. She said the pastor might be next. An interview could help us unravel the Little Clementine slayings." Leo pulled out his phone and started his recording app to cover all their bases. Considering the girls' behavior, he wasn't inclined to go in without some kind of backup. "Let's go talk to them."

Before Vance could agree or disagree, Leo was caught around the middle by Maybelle, who appeared between the trees and hugged herself tight against his chest, batting her eyelashes at him.

"Agent Ambrose, why didn't you join the service?" she purred.

Leo shoved his hands between her arms and his body, trying to pry himself loose.

"Let him go, Maybelle." Vance's tone was all seriousness. It reminded Leo of Papu's "stern" tone back when Leo broke Yaya's vase.

But the girl was slicker than an eel in twisting around him, one of her thin legs running up and down his calf in a way that made his stomach turn. She was *fifteen*.

"Maybelle. This isn't appropriate. Maybelle, please step away."

Assisted by Vance's strong grip on her upper arms, the girl disengaged from Leo. Though she didn't get the message.

She put her hands on her hips, standing within Leo's personal space.

Straightening his coat, Leo gulped a breath of fresh air and curbed the curses he wanted to spit at her. "Maybelle, I need to ask you about what you and your sister were just discussing. What Agent Jessup and I overheard."

The girl pouted deeper. A puff of breath steamed up between them.

"What kind of time did you spend with Chet Crawford and Ernie Murray?"

Maybelle rolled her eyes, throwing her chin in the air. "What do you think? We had sex, obviously. A lot of it too. We know what we're doing now."

She stopped there, but a smile came to her lips.

Considering the secretive nature of the town…maybe she really didn't know right from wrong when it came to sexual relations and consent.

"Don't you think something might be strange about that?" Leo kept his voice gentle, wondering if the persona the girl had adopted was an act. "Chet and Ernie were both almost fifty, older than your mom. You know that, right? And you're a minor. You're fifteen."

Maybelle shrugged. "That's just the way things are around here." Stepping in closer, making him back up because he did not want to touch her, she met his eyes and winked. "When in Rome, do as the Romans do. Meanwhile, I sure gotta get back inside to the service before someone thinks the axe murderer found me."

Leo gritted his teeth. "Where's your sister?"

She shrugged again. "I bet she's run on home. She might be there all by herself for a while." She winked at him. "See you later, I hope?"

Before Leo could find his voice again, the girl turned tail and ran, her too-short church dress flipping up into the air behind her. Turning away, he leaned back against the tree.

Vance grunted, his disgust as plain as could be. "This town is something else."

34

Back at the community center, Emma fixed herself a cup of coffee at the makeshift refreshments station. Basically, it was a coffeepot, some sugar, creamer, and stirring sticks. If she closed her eyes, she could almost pretend she was back in D.C., as long as she ignored the chill air, buzzing fluorescents, and single wobbly table. No biggie.

Bringing Sheriff Lowell up to speed on the alleged sexual assaults was understandable. But Mia could take the lead right now. Emma didn't need to rehear what Vance and Leo had reported—they'd immediately briefed her and Mia on the Sweeney teens outside the church.

Emma couldn't imagine how the men on her team had felt on overhearing two teens openly discuss being raped. *And while hanging out on a damn swing set, of all places.* The fact that the girls hadn't called it rape only made the situation worse.

Sheriff Lowell took a seat, as if the weight of all this new information was too heavy to hold standing up.

Jacinda headed over to the board as Emma resumed her

seat. "All right, so who do we think appears most suspect at this point?"

Emma gestured with her coffee at the gaping space on the board beneath the word *Suspects*. . "Plenty of women in this community could've wanted vengeance against Bud. And there's quite the generational difference, considering all three of our male victims. Bud's, Chet's, and Ernie's victims could be decades apart in age."

Denae crossed one leg over her other. "Whoever axed these men, assuming it was the same person, knows about all the abuse."

"Plenty of community men might also feel protective of their women." Vance sat with his arms and legs crossed, seeming to shield himself from the cold community-center air. "Wade Somerson may want payback for injury to his wife."

Jacinda wrote Wade's name on the board.

"April Sweeney seems to think Pastor Darl is next." Leo headed over to the cooler of bottled waters a kind community member had provided. "Bud was his father, remember? It tracks that Dad may have taught the son. But I don't think Ian Darl is continuing the family tradition."

"Think that's why he's moving?" Emma sipped her coffee. It was hotter than anything else. "And Julianna knew about the abuse. She told us about Lizbet."

"If Louise and Rosemary were killed for remaining silent about their husbands' crimes, then Julianna could be a target too." Leo unscrewed the cap on his water bottle.

"Cora Hardy knew too," Mia pointed out. "Even if her husband's clueless."

Emma thought out loud. "Maybe Julianna or Cora took matters into their own hands?"

"Or did their families?" Leo asked. "Maybe Lizbet told her husband, Bo? Maybe Julianna told Ian?"

Denae bit off a humorless laugh. "Don't stop there with the hypotheticals, people. For all we know, Ian and Bo were victims too. The photos seemed to be all female, but anything that can happen to a little girl can happen to a little boy."

Jacinda's chalk pencil squeaked as she finished writing Ian Darl's name on the chalkboard. She frowned and leaned against the wall, tapping the pencil on her arm. "We have a lot of suspects but not a lot of information to make one better than the next. That what I'm hearing as the consensus?"

Emma sighed. "Yeah, pretty much. But Wade Somerson checks a lot of boxes. His wife was assaulted, he lives alone, he was the last known person to speak with all the victims… except Bud. Maybe our first lead was the best lead after all? No one's been able to find Wade Somerson since the first day we were here. Has he gone into hiding or what?"

The group was quiet for a moment, thinking.

Leo sat back down in his seat, staring at all the names on the board. "And we have no way of knowing if Louise or Rosemary knew. These women were married to the perverts. Slept in the same beds with them every night. Secrets like this are hard to keep."

"There'd be a whisper network among women in a town like this," said Mia. Emma knew she was thinking of their conversations about and with Lizbet, who clearly knew more than she'd let on. "I think getting Lizbet's name is proof of that. Seems like a fair bet that every woman in town knows… or knew…what was happening, even if they weren't victims. After what Leo and Vance saw, I'd wager the whisper network transcends generations too."

Beside her, Vance grunted and sipped his coffee. His normally relaxed face was pinched into a frown, as had been the case since they'd met back up outside the church. "So everyone knows, and everyone's covering it up. Great.

Murders aside, this whole town's culpable for what's been happening to the little ones."

As the coffee burned through her dry throat, Emma wished she could disagree. But he was right. This whole town was guilty.

Jacinda frowned, setting the pencil into the board's chalk tray. "Unfortunately, endless interviewing is getting us nowhere. Each round of interviews just compounds the mess of information and suspects we've got."

"Unearthing all these secrets is worth something." Denae's eyes roved around the group. "We're collecting puzzle pieces but don't yet have enough pieced together to see the whole picture."

"We're not even close to done." Emma sighed and swallowed the last of her coffee. "What Vance just said is right. There's a lot of blame to go around. Even though Maybelle was pretty cavalier and vocal about having sex with older men, what do her parents think about it? Or all the girls' parents, for that matter? Add them to the suspect list too."

Jacinda shook her head. "I'm not writing all forty-plus citizens on the board."

"We've all seen the *not in my backyard* folks do an about-face when it matters," Vance agreed. "Maybe the parents were just fine with what was going on right up until it was their own little girls getting the…" He growled low in his throat.

"What?" Mia nudged his elbow.

He shook his head. "I can't find a way to finish that sentence that's not gonna make me want to take an axe to a few people myself. Y'all know what I mean."

Sheriff Lowell coughed, seeming to wake himself from the stupor he'd sat in on the edge of their circle. "I think that's about all the conjecture I can take for one night. How about you start bringing people into the actual police station over in Zeigler City for official interrogations, interviews, or whatever you want to call 'em at this stage?"

Jacinda combed her fingers through her hair as she peered at the board. "We have motive, and out of a sea of suspects, someone will crack under pressure. Let's all get out of here for now and get some sleep. Tomorrow's a new day. However, I need a couple of you to keep an eye on our potential Darl targets."

"I'll do it." Emma and Leo volunteered simultaneously.

Emma stood but remained near the board. She snapped an updated photo with her iPad before walking away from the day's work. She'd review the image and check it against her notes before bed. All the information, right down to the distances between crime scenes and the various suspects' homes, needed to be in her head when morning came.

One way or another, they were going to find the killer.

35

A half hour or so later, Leo was doing his best to ignore the amorphous stain on the bedside motel carpet as he pulled on jeans and buckled his belt. Next came his vest and shoulder holster.

The bedroom was so quiet and warm, the very air seemed to judge him for abandoning it to venture out into the night…but action was the only thing that made sense. He couldn't leave someone else to die by an axe-wielding maniac if he could help it.

Not even a pervert of the highest order.

Lizbet's confession of the wrongs done to her was monumental. It was the kind of admission a person offered up on their deathbed.

Even though he'd volunteered to protect the Darls, he couldn't help but think about Lizbet Sweeney Somerson. He would follow through on his agreed task and stake out the Darl property with Emma. But first, he'd conduct a simple wellness check at the Somerson household.

Emma said Lizbet was never directly asked about it before, not by anyone. Never pushed to confess what Bud had done to her. There was no way she came out of that conversation with Mia and Emma unscathed.

She had to go back to her new husband and daughters...would she tell them? Admit what had happened? If not...she's probably crawling out of her own skin right about now.

And what if the daughters confessed to Lizbet about what they'd endured? Maybelle had said she was "bored without Chet and Ernie around." How would Lizbet react to such an attitude? He hadn't seen her attempt to change anything about the way the girls presented themselves. It stood to reason she was well aware of what was happening and simply felt powerless to stop it.

Leo couldn't stop thinking about the expression on Mia's face when Emma had described the interview. Mia was worried about Lizbet tonight, not the murderer.

Which made Leo think that maybe there was something real to worry about with her.

Because after what had happened to Lizbet, plus the agony of confessing, all while knowing she hadn't been able to save her daughters from the same fate...would it be so far-fetched to believe that Lizbet felt ready to die?

I'm not resting without doing a wellness check.

Leo finished tying his bootlaces and grabbed his coat from the hook on the door. The worry that the broken woman would harm herself was more than he could live with.

Better to get out of here and check on her at some point during their protective stakeout.

He crept by the other agents' rooms, not wanting to disturb them.

At the front door, he looked around for Emma. But she either wasn't ready or was already waiting near one of the Expeditions.

Leo hurried toward the attached gravel lot where a single

streetlight cast a hazy glow over the Bureau vehicles. As he neared their convoy, a shadow shifted.

What the...

The shadow stepped out from a clump of trees at the edge of the lot, full and human and right in his path.

His Glock was in his hand as he stepped back. "FBI! Identify yourself and step into the light with your hands where I can see them."

"Sorry! It's me." Emma's apology cut through the silence in a shout-whisper. She stepped into the edge of the streetlight's halo with her hands in front of her. "Didn't mean to scare you."

He holstered his weapon and scowled. "Dammit, Emma, I thought you were a fucking ghost!"

She went oddly wide-eyed for a moment before grinning. "Sorry. Really. I should've called out before stepping out. What were you gonna do, though? Shoot a ghost?"

"Ha." He took a deep breath, chuckling. "It couldn't hurt. Point is, I didn't know what or who you were. Don't do that again, all right?"

She tucked her hair back into her winter cap, nodding. "I'll do my best. You ready?"

Just like him, she appeared ready to go. Early.

As he explained his rationale for checking on Lizbet first, Emma nodded along. When he'd finished, she offered a deep sigh and faced the highway leading into Little Clementine. "I was kind of thinking the same thing. She's had a tough night on top of a tough life. I was planning on stopping by her place first thing in the morning."

"Or we could check tonight." Leo eyed her, waiting for the decision he guessed was coming.

"Or we could check tonight. After we make sure the Darls are snug as bugs in rugs." She grinned, tilting her head.

"I like the way you think, Last."

"Back at ya, Ambrose. So…you wanna drive?"

"Hell yes, I do."

Leaving the Expedition's lights off as he backed out, Leo kept his foot light on the gas until he was on the highway, then he accelerated steadily.

"Don't we want to get there tonight, Grandpa?"

"Shut it, Mario Andretti."

When they arrived at the Darl homestead, every room appeared occupied. Light glowed from multiple windows, shining through thin gaps in the curtains. Leo lifted a pair of binoculars from the back seat.

"Julianna Darl is in the bedroom. Looks like she's on the phone."

"And the good pastors, father and son?"

"Gregory Darl…living room. I can only see his legs, but he just crossed them, so he's still alive."

"Or our axe murderer is also a puppeteer."

Leo stifled a laugh. Now was not the time to relax and lose focus. They were close on their killer's tail and would have her soon enough.

"Looks like Ian Darl is unaccounted for. No…wait. He's in the dining room. Can't see much of him, but I have movement. As of now, the remaining Darl family members are alive and well and in their home."

Emma mumbled another snide comment, and Leo let himself laugh this time. The Darls were safe and sound. He could let himself relax, a little.

Together, he and Emma sat watching the Darl family for an hour.

"Quiet night in for these three." Emma bit back a yawn. She peered through the binoculars, then dropped them. "Want to go do that wellness check on Lizbet real fast?"

Leo didn't need to be asked twice. He put the SUV in gear. "Absolutely."

"And I do mean fast."

He rolled his eyes and headed out.

※

THE SOMERSON HOME loomed out from the darkness ahead. He'd brought them to the property in under five minutes, and without exceeding the speed limit. Still, he noticed Emma's right leg jittering, like she was pressing it repeatedly into the floorboard.

"You sure it's okay that I'm driving?"

"We made it here before sunup, so I guess I won't file any complaints with Jacinda."

He accelerated up the drive just enough to put a grin on her face. Lights blazed from nearly every window in the little wood-framed cabin, as if someone inside were scared of the dark.

The hairs on Leo's neck rose, and a cold sweat broke out on his skin. "Seem strange to you that the lights are on?"

"You bet it does."

Place like Little Clementine, the lights aren't on this late like this without good reason.

Leo hit the front walk at a fast pace, Emma right on his heels.

He'd barely knocked before Bo threw open the door.

"What's happened? Where is she?" The skin around Bo's eyes was red and puffy, like he'd been rubbing away tears or sleep. Stepping outside, the man babbled on before Leo could attempt an answer. "I don't want the girls to hear. They're right inside, freaking out like nobody's business. Just tell me, okay? I knew I should've kept her from going out, but she's been so upset. Come on, tell me!"

Leo waved for the man to slow down, trying to catch up. Why the hell hadn't he called them if he was this worried?

"Whoa, whoa. Calm down, please. Nothing's happened to Lizbet as far as we know."

Leo traded glances with Emma before leading Bo Somerson to the side of the house, encouraging him to sit down on the porch bench beside some dead ferns. "Now, what are you saying? When did your wife leave the house tonight?"

The man breathed deeply, rocking on the seat as he stared at the planks on the porch. "A while ago. Twenty minutes? Half an hour? I thought about going out to look for her, but with the girls here and the murders happening…" He broke off, his voice choking. "Lizbet'd never forgive me if I went off to find her and something happened to Maybelle and April in the meantime. I was just wondering if I should call the sheriff when y'all pulled up."

"That's why we're here. To help. We'll figure this out." Emma rested one hand on his shoulder.

"Wait…" The man straightened where he sat, his eyes narrowing. "If nothing happened to Lizbet, what are you two doing here?"

Man, these people were suspicious of Feds. Leo perched on the bench seat at Somerson's side. "We only came to do a sort of…wellness check on her. Make sure she was all right. We had no way of knowing she wouldn't be here."

"A wellness check? Why?" he demanded. "Isn't that something you do for gray-haired grannies who might be having heart attacks?"

"We'll explain everything later." Emma was firm in her explanation. "But for now, we should focus on finding Lizbet. Where is she likely to go?"

"To Julianna Darl's." Bo glanced back at the front door, then shook his head as if debating with himself. "Everyone's been murdered in their sleep, right? 'Cept for Rosemary, who was wandering around outside her home?"

Leo nodded, already guessing where this was going.

Maybelle emerged from the front door wearing her nightdress, such as it was. Leo turned his head.

"Why hello, Agent Ambrose. What's going on, Daddy?"

"Get back in the house. You and your sister are to stay here, behind a locked door, until I get back with your mom."

The girl pouted, then paled and retreated as she took in her stepfather's glare. "Okay. I'll be inside. With April, like you said."

Bo turned back to the agents. "All right, then the girls'll be fine. Their heads are on straight enough to keep inside the house. And they know how to use a gun, anyhow. Maybelle! April! Lock the door behind me. I'm going with the agents to find your mom. Shoot anyone who tries to get in."

"On it!" April screamed back.

36

Emma stepped out of the Expedition onto the Darls' gravel driveway—which was now empty of Gregory's gray Buick LeSabre. The house appeared empty as well. The bedroom and living room were dark. One sign of life remained. Ian Darl still sat in the dining room, scribbling away. "How long were we gone?"

"Twelve minutes." Leo joined her on the gravel. "Let's go see where the parental figures went."

Behind them, Bo hopped out and followed. Emma debated the wisdom of bringing him along. The Darls could've gone to bed. Lizbet clearly wasn't here, so Bo's relevance was diminished.

Seeing how shaken and fearful he was, she chose to ignore his tagging along. It would take more energy than she currently possessed to get him back inside the vehicle.

The trio arrived on the Darls' porch, and Leo pounded the door. It was a solid "cop knock," which would've awakened the dead. "Pastor Darl? Mrs. Darl? This is Agent Leo Ambrose and Agent Emma Last. We need to speak with you."

A light came on, and Ian opened the door. His expression

was a mix of fear and curiosity. "Agents? What can I do for you?"

Emma didn't feel like remaining courteous. "Where are your parents?"

"They were called away. Someone needed guidance."

"Was it Lizbet?" Bo stepped around Leo's shoulder.

It was as if a shot of electricity jumped across the porch. The two men stared at each other for just a split second too long. A small flush grew from under Bo's collar.

From the way Leo glanced from one man to the other, she knew he'd caught the chemistry as well.

"Yeah, Bo, yeah." No one could've missed the tenderness in the way Ian spoke Bo's name. "It was Lizbet. I thought my parents were on their way to your place. I guess not?"

"No. And Lizbet left about twenty minutes ago. Maybe longer."

Emma turned to Leo. "Julianna had to be talking to Lizbet on the phone in the bedroom. They must've agreed to meet somewhere."

Rather than ask everyone inside, Ian stepped out into the cold. "Yeah, that's right. Lizbet called and talked to Mom. Then Mom asked Dad to drive her out to the cliffs."

"No," Bo nearly shouted. "Julianna wouldn't bring your dad. Lizbet wouldn't want him there. She'd only want to talk to Julianna."

Emma stepped down from the porch. Standing in the gravel drive, she pointed at the porch steps. "Sit." The two young men, used to years of obeying authority, sat obediently. "I'm done with the secrets, gentlemen. It's time to tell us everything you know, who else might know what you know, and anything else you think might be pertinent. Bo, tell me why Lizbet wouldn't want anything to do with Pastor Gregory Darl."

Before answering, Bo cast an apologetic glance at Ian, who only nodded encouragement. "She's right. Time to tell."

Bo took a deep breath. "Pastor Gregory, Chet Crawford, and Ernie Murray have been molesting the girls of the parish."

"My grandfather too." Ian's face was pale as the moonlight, as if the truth were taking all his power with it. "My grandfather taught them how. He was the ringleader."

Leo's voice rose darkly from the porch. "And no one thought to report it?"

"God and family before outsiders." Ian recited the words like a mantra. "'But I would have you know, that the head of every man is Christ; and the head of the woman is the man.' First Corinthians 11:3." He looked up at Emma. "Heaven help you if you are a little girl in Little Clementine."

"Or if you're a man who loves another man? Tell me about this." Emma twirled a finger between the pair of them.

Instead of running away from another truth like she expected, Bo lifted his chin. "We fell in love when we were younger."

At the word *love*, tears pooled in Ian's eyes.

Emma recognized the feeling. Loss. He bowed his head, and her view of his emotional turmoil was lost to the shadows.

Maybe he's praying.

Bo continued, seeming as pained as his first love. "My dad caught us kissing behind our garage. He sent me away to a reform school, hoping the gay would go away, I guess. My mom never really forgave him. I was away when she got sick, and it was so fast. She died before I could come back. But I think I got off light compared to Ian."

"I saw a photo of you two in your dresser." Leo stood above them, arms crossed, but the cold anger in his voice had mellowed a bit.

The pastor's son had curled into himself, but his muffled voice held a note of surprise and sadness that was difficult to witness. "You kept that?"

Bo shrugged. "Of course." As if keeping a picture of your forbidden teenage love in a town like Little Clementine was perfectly normal.

"How did your dad handle it, Ian?" Emma almost didn't want to ask.

"I was to whip myself with the cat-o'-nine-tails almost every night, to ensure any impure thoughts were expunged before bed. I still do it. He supervises." Ian shrugged down a sleeve, revealing a recently scabbed-over shoulder.

"Dear God help us," Bo muttered.

Ian let the material fall back into place. "Back then, though, he read me multiple Bible verses while I tortured myself. And he disowned me. I watched him cross my name off the will myself. He also told me, very recently, that I was unfit to lead his heavenly flock. Between that and Bo's marriage, I had no more reason to stay in Little Clementine. So I put first and last month's rent on an apartment in Baltimore and told my parents I was leaving."

"Pastor Gregory Darl is the ungodly one." Anger, old and venomous, dripped from Bo Somerson's words. "My mother told me what he'd done to her. She told me to steer clear of him. I tried."

"Wait. *Gregory* Darl hurt Lizbet too?" Emma wasn't sure she heard correctly.

Bo glanced at Ian before answering. "Yeah. That's why I agreed to marry her. They don't touch married women."

Emma rubbed her eyes, as if she could block out the images coming to mind. She didn't understand how these two men, who were victims of these criminals as much as the women, weren't killing everyone around them. She knew only the tip of the iceberg, and she was half tempted to grab an axe too.

"Do you think Lizbet would be capable of killing the men who hurt her? Vengeance? Maybe a way to protect her girls?"

Though her girls were already so, so hurt...maybe that was what triggered her.

But both men shook their heads.

"Lizbet doesn't even kill spiders. There's no way she'd do anything like this." Bo was insistent.

"Would your dad?" Emma immediately worried her blunt question would stop Bo cold.

But Bo shook his head. "My dad's a broken man. There might've been a time earlier when he would have been... tough." The word lingered in the air for a moment, and Emma knew Bo had dealt with a lot from his father. "But even if he felt vengeful, he headed off on a camping trip to New Hampshire a few days ago. 'To get away from the drama,' he said."

"You didn't think to mention this earlier?" Leo asked.

"I just found out tonight, actually. He was out of the mountains and had service again. He called to see how things were going."

All that information was easy enough to check. Emma bit back a sigh. "So in your opinion, neither your wife nor your dad would want...*justice*, let's say, for what happened in the past?

There was the briefest hesitation before Ian spoke up. "My mom would."

Emma's heart rate revved up.

All along, they'd expected someone to break and spill all the deep, dark stories. This was the moment they'd been waiting for during their whole investigation.

"Why do you say that?"

"My grandfather raped my mother. My father's disowned

me. She's been acting strangely ever since I told her I was moving. I thought it was just empty-nest syndrome, you know? She keeps talking about how lonely she is. How she'll be all alone. I keep trying to reassure her. But she says she deserves to be alone because she's allowed so many people to be hurt." He hesitated. "But she's angry."

"How do you know?"

"I know my mom."

Emma squeezed his arm. "Tell me where they went."

37

We parked beside Lizbet's vehicle. The good girl was already here. She always was one to follow directions. I'd worried she might get lost taking the twisting road through the hillside forest, but she knew the place I'd described. It was where I always came to do my thinking, when I needed to be alone with only God and His creation.

"Why are we meeting out here?"

I shook my head ever so slightly. My dear husband seemed put out, but I couldn't say that I felt any sympathy for him. His question had so many possible answers.

We're meeting out here because I don't want to bloody my own house.

We're meeting out here because I want Lizbet to know she and her girls are now safe.

We're meeting out here because I want to protect my son.

We're here for deliverance. For my last vendetta.

But mostly, we were meeting out here because I wanted to hack my husband to death with an axe, and I wanted to have the room to swing with every ounce of strength I possessed.

The flat overlook at the end of the trees gave me all that and more. Once I had him near the edge, he'd be forced to run toward my axe, or fling himself over the cliffside.

Oh, how I prayed he would choose to run my way.

He cleared his throat beside me. "I asked you a question, Julianna. Now, please, tell me the purpose for our meeting out here. And remember, all things under God's Heaven are known to Him and made known to those who serve Him in their hearts. No lie shall go unpunished."

Soon, I'll never have to hear his hypocritical preaching again.

"It's a pleasant night, Gregory. I asked her here so that we could look at the stars and know that we are minuscule in God's great plan."

He grunted. "It's January. Your definition of pleasant and mine are clearly different."

We have different definitions regarding many things.

"Pop the trunk. I'll pull out the blanket."

A small *thunk* told me he'd used the fob to pop the back. I stepped out into the night, letting the breeze brush away the lightest sheen of sweat from my forehead.

Tonight was the night. All the hurt, all the betrayal, all the trauma would go away. A burst of adrenaline made my hands tremble. With my other deliverances, there'd always been a strange calm, a sense of resolution. Knowing I was about to deliver my husband from God's earth, well, it felt different.

I had thought to offer him more moonshine, the last of his poisoned punch. How fitting it would be to watch the light of recognition shine forth when I showed him which bottle I had poured from. It was the same bottle I had poured from the other night, ensuring he and our son slept soundly while I carried out my grisly task not a hundred feet away.

I brought that bottle with me tonight, anticipating the moment when Gregory's eyes would begin to droop, just before I raised my axe to end him once and for all. But now, with my heart racing, I realized I wanted him to see it happen, to be fully conscious and aware. Like his father had been.

Gregory and Bud had always known exactly what they were doing when they plundered the innocence of so many young girls. Why should I provide any semblance of mercy to my husband in delivering his death? I lifted the trunk.

There sat all the tools a person would need if they were stranded on the side of the road. A woolen blanket, a small spade to dig tires out of muddy tracks, extra bottles of oil, windshield-wiper fluid, and a bottle of moonshine wrapped in an old shirt, alongside an axe.

"Hurry up," Gregory demanded. He'd already taken a few steps into the trees that separated the parking area from the overlook.

"Coming." I lifted the axe and bottle and draped the woolen blanket over them. No reason to startle him before the appropriate time.

I was ashamed to admit, even to myself, that I probably would've let Gregory and his brothers in sin continue their depraved ways if Gregory hadn't disowned Ian. My own guilt burned in my chest. But I was making up for my passivity now.

If all went according to plan, Gregory, the last of the molesters, would be gone. Lizbet would be reassured she and her daughters were safe. If Lizbet felt secure, she would release Bo from his sham of a marriage. Then Bo and Ian could lead the flock further into the twenty-first century, protecting all the children. And Ian would stay in Little Clementine, with me, for always.

The light sheen of sweat returned, chilling me.

I stepped toward Lizbet, calling her name. She stood looking out over the cliff's edge, no doubt glorying in the beauty of the creation before her, just as I had done so many times myself. As I called to her a second time, she turned with a small smile of greeting. A smile that immediately disappeared as she spotted Gregory approaching.

"What are you doing here? Julianna, I said I wanted to speak to you."

"That's a fine way to greet your pastor. You're the one calling for spiritual guidance, for the word of the Lord in the middle of the night. I've answered your call."

Lizbet fell silent. Tears pricked at the younger woman's eyes.

I ignored my husband's irritated bluster. "It's all right, Lizbet. I promise you. It will all be all right from now on." Pivoting around behind her, I was careful to keep the axe vertical behind Lizbet's back while also holding the bottle clutched between my arm and hip. With my free hand, I draped the blanket around her shoulders.

Gregory's mouth fell open. "I thought you were getting the blanket for me."

Stepping out from behind Lizbet, I retrieved the bottle and held it out. The shirt slipped away as I dropped the axe to my side, just as I had so many times before. Perspiration forced me to readjust my grip.

Until this point, Rosemary was the only one who faced me before she died. Gregory had several inches on her and about fifty pounds. It'd take more strength to batter him down. But I would…or I would die trying.

The moment my dear husband saw the weapon, he froze.

I let the bottle fall, relishing the sound of shattering glass as the last of Gregory Darl's foul medicine soaked into the rocks and dirt at my feet.

It was with great satisfaction that I watched the realization come over his face. His eyes, which I'd looked into for over three decades, widened. The mouth I'd kissed opened into a large *O*.

And me? I smiled.

But I spoke to Lizbet. "Dear one, please forgive me for not protecting you or your girls. As the pastor's wife, it was my duty to protect my flock, not leave you to the wolves. I know I'm late, and that I'm undeserving, but I ask your forgiveness nonetheless. Removing these perpetrators will not heal the hurt, but I hope it will protect other innocents in the future."

Gregory stepped to the side, so we now faced each other across the open dirt, with the cliff edge to my right and his left.

"Julianna Darl! What have you done? You…you killed men of God, men who are invested in this community, who love the mem—"

"Who love the members a bit too much, Pastor." I practically spat the last word as I stepped to my left, grinning as I watched my damn fool of a husband pivot to match my move.

He now stood with his back to the cliff. Maybe fifteen feet separated him from a drop that would end his days. And yet I could not imagine allowing him such a mercy. His actions had driven a wedge into our marriage, and into our community as a whole.

Just so, my axe would be like a wedge between him and his grasp on life in this earthly realm. Miraculously, whatever nerves had been threatening to overtake me so far had vanished. A rush of certainty pulsed through my blood. What happened to him was between him and the Lord. And I would arrange that meeting.

I stepped toward him.

He stumbled back, now just a few paces from the cliff's edge. "God will never forgive you, Julianna. God is to man what man is to woman. You're going against the natural and celestial order. Put that thing down, beg forgiveness, and we'll move on from here."

Lizbet stepped away from me, but I wasn't sure if it was uncertainty or fear guiding her. She moved behind Gregory, using him as a shield, or so it seemed, but it put her closer to the edge of the cliff too. She didn't understand I wouldn't hurt her. I was here to protect her. She didn't need my vile husband to do it.

For the moment, however, I couldn't focus on her.

"There's no moving on from here, Pastor Darl. Not after you disinherited my son, not after you condemned who he is, not after you took him from me. But I'm going to get him back. Yes. I will not be left alone in this hellscape with you as my only company. I'm going to make this place better. A true Christian village led by a loving, kind pastor. My son."

Gregory's face was pale, but he wasn't scared. Milky white was the color he turned when he was furious.

"No." But the word held no conviction. No bluster.

"After you're dead, this town will be safe. Lizbet!" I glanced at the scared woman. She wouldn't be scared much longer, poor thing. "You and your daughters will be safe. There will be no need to live a lie with Bo. You can be free. And he can be free to be with Ian—"

"I will not allow that abomination near my flock!" Gregory roared and rushed toward me.

But I did not step back. I raised my axe, ready to send him to the gates of Hell.

38

"Coordinates confirmed. ETA fifteen minutes." SSA Jacinda Hollingsworth's voice confirmed their call for backup as Emma took a hairpin turn up to the cliffs above Little Clementine. Bo and Ian had both described the place as a quiet refuge at the top of a winding forest road. People in the town called it "the overlook" and often used it as a place for solitary reflection or communion with God.

Except someone now intended to use the location to commit an act of grisly murder.

Trees scratched at the exterior of the Expedition, like werewolves clawing for entrance. Emma ignored the environment, keeping her eyes dead ahead on the dirt road leading up and up.

"This whole thing could be done in fifteen minutes." Emma tried not to sound pessimistic, but it was a hard thing. Leo disconnected without comment.

They'd left Bo and Ian at the Darl house, telling the pair they'd let them know when everything was settled.

Dust swirled in front of Emma's headlights. It was like

driving through brown fog. She ran some windshield fluid, flicking on the wipers to swipe the glass clean.

"I think we're near the top. I'm turning off the headlights. I don't want to draw attention."

"Just be careful." Leo's tone was tight, but whenever she stole a glance his way, his face was attentive and open.

The world outside went dark. Emma used the full moon and the bright stars to guide her into a gravel parking area. There was so much more light out here than in D.C., with the Milky Way umbrellaing above them.

Two cars were already in the makeshift parking lot.

"That's the Darls' car. Bet the other one belongs to the Somersons."

Emma completed the count in her head. "Two Darls and Lizbet. The cars are empty, so they've stepped out somewhere."

Leo shot her a glance. "Vest tight? Gun ready?"

"Locked and loaded."

"Then watch your step. Follow me through the tree line."

"Roger that." Emma opened her door and stepped out. A wisp of cold air snaked down the neck of her vest. She rounded the front of the Expedition, stepping carefully to keep silent.

Leo led the way, veering right, looping through the barren maple trees and the thin line of spruce, the piney needles smelling of Christmas. Emma kept an eye out for errant roots, which could trip her.

Voices grew louder as they approached an opening in the trees. A small clearing of dirt and random rocks spread out before them. Then the grayish dirt ended in a pit of black—the edge of the cliff.

Two figures stood right at the lip. One blast of wind, and Lizbet Somerson and Pastor Gregory Darl would be falling into darkness to never return.

Or from one swing of an axe blade.

Julianna Darl stood before the pair. The axe blade flashed in the moonlight as she twisted the handle, re-gripping the haft.

"We need to flank her." Emma whispered instructions to Leo. "I'll go left and take the body. You go right and disarm."

"Got it." He stepped forward, breaking through the cover of the trees. Julianna did not appear to see him.

Emma followed, Glock raised.

Pastor Gregory's voice was filled with righteous fury as he quoted the "rules" Ian had stated only a few minutes earlier at the Darl house.

"God will never forgive you. God is to man what man is to woman. You're going against the natural and celestial order. Put that thing down, beg forgiveness, and we'll move on from here."

Lizbet Somerson made eye contact with Emma and took the slightest step away from Julianna, getting behind the pastor. If she stepped back any farther, however, she'd risk going over the edge. Emma held up a hand, silently telling Lizbet to stop. The woman froze as instructed.

Julianna was having none of her husband's preaching. "There's no moving on from here, Pastor Darl. Not after you disinherited my son, not after you condemned who he is, not after you took him from me. But I'm going to get him back. Yes. I will not be left alone in this hellscape with you as my only company. I'm going to make this place better. A true Christian village led by a loving, kind pastor. My son."

The woman's words registered with Emma. Ian was right. Guilt and rage fueled his mother. All those tangled emotions were on full display.

Together, Emma and Leo approached Julianna from their designated sides. Emma kept her eyes on the axe. If Julianna lunged, they'd have milliseconds to stop her.

"After you're dead, this town will be safe. Lizbet!" Julianna pleaded for understanding. "You and your daughters will be safe. There will be no need to live a lie with Bo. You can be free. He can be free to be with Ian—"

She has a whole dreamland plan.

Emma holstered her weapon. She'd need both hands free if she were going to tackle Julianna and keep her restrained.

Almost there.

Gregory Darl had seen them by now too, and apparently had gained some confidence. He screamed at his axe-wielding wife. "I will not allow that abomination near my flock!"

He took two steps forward as Julianna swung the axe upward. Gregory faltered, his eyes wide with shock or the recognition that the woman he believed he controlled actually had a mind of her own. Gregory Darl skidded to a stop before his wife.

The axe arced down, and Emma thought she would be too late. She raced forward, ready to tackle Julianna, who heard her. The pastor's wife spun, holding the axe over her head. Emma put her hands up, ready to deflect the weapon if Julianna struck.

Leo was there first, rushing in from the side to grab the tool above Julianna's grip. He wrenched at it, but Julianna would not let go. She struggled against him as Emma came forward. She looped a leg around Julianna's, sweeping the woman onto her back and going down with her to pin her to the ground.

Emma's jaw connected with the axe handle as they smacked onto the ground in a tangle. Julianna tried using her weapon to shove Emma away. Emma reached for the woman's elbows, controlling her arms so she couldn't bring the axe-head down. Leo seized the tool, finally twisting it from Julianna's grip.

Blood rushing through her ears, Emma rolled Julianna over as she climbed on top of her and knelt, yanking her handcuffs off her belt and securing her. "Julianna Darl, you are under arrest for four counts of murder. Stay still."

Julianna didn't fight. She swiveled her head to look sideways at Emma. "You don't know what you've done. He's evil."

"I've done my job. And he'll be going to court too. Don't fret."

"What?" Gregory's voice rose like a whirlwind. "I'm the victim here. This woman murdered two of my friends. Two righteous men and their wives. And my father! She left a toddler an orphan."

"Better an orphan than raised by sinners." Julianna spoke quietly, as if she only wanted Emma to hear and understand.

Leo kicked the axe across the clearing. "You are under arrest as well, sir. Multiple counts of rape and molestation."

"I did nothing wrong. I raise my flock using God's commandments."

"Julianna?"

Everyone stopped as Lizbet called the pastor's wife's name.

Julianna lifted her head the inch that she could. "Yes, Lizbet?"

"I forgive you."

Lizbet stood straight. Stronger.

Emma and Leo understood Lizbet's intention at the same time, sharing a look of concern that morphed into dark understanding

Lizbet rushed forward, the skirt of her dress a fluttering wing in the night.

And she shoved Pastor Gregory Darl over the cliff.

Emma and Leo dove, but both were too late.

A howl of fear and terror rose through the chilly air. It

echoed off the cliff face until it was abruptly stifled by a horrible, wet *thump*.

Silence draped across the starry night, and the only sound Emma heard was her own heartbeat.

39

Swirls of red-and-blue lights shifted through the clifftop trees as relief flooded through Emma. The sirens were harsh and grating after the eerie quiet following Gregory Darl's fall, but the sound meant she and Leo were no longer alone.

As the light chased away the darkness, Leo escorted a handcuffed Lizbet in the direction of the parking lot.

They set the two women side by side in the dirt, backs against their Expedition's rear wheel, and waited for backup to arrive. Neither woman had spoken another word since Gregory Darl was pushed to his death. Emma imagined both Lizbet and Julianna had a lot of practice remaining silent and obedient, and she had no desire to break their quiet. She'd heard enough for tonight.

The sirens stopped. In the lot, what sounded like a million footsteps scrambled toward them.

"Over here!" Emma called out. Her ears were ringing—either from the quiet or the noise.

Federal agents and law enforcement emerged before them like ghosts. SSA Jacinda Hollingsworth rushed toward her people, and Emma was happy to see her. "You two all right?"

"We've caught the perpetrator, Jacinda." Emma gestured to the two handcuffed women sitting in the dirt. "Julianna Darl committed the axe murders in Little Clementine. However, we were unable to save Pastor Gregory Darl. He was pushed over the edge of the cliff by Lizbet Sweeney Somerson as we were tackling and cuffing Julianna and securing the weapon."

Jacinda's eyebrows lifted, and for a second, Emma thought she spotted a flash of respect cross the SSA's expression. "What else?"

"There's also some broken glass up there, which may contain traces of a drug that had been used to incapacitate Gregory and Ian Darl on the night Bud Darl was murdered. It's probably the same drug used to incapacitate teenage girls in Little Clementine. The elder pastors here were both sexual predators, as were the other male victims, Chet and Ernie. Julianna Darl engaged in a mission of vengeance for her mistreatment, and that of most other women in this community."

Jacinda's eyebrows shot up to her hairline. But she didn't press for further details. "I look forward to the report. For now, you both look like hell. Transfer Mrs. Darl and Mrs. Somerson to Sheriff Lowell's people. Then sit out for a hot second. You've had a busy night."

"Understood, Jacinda. Thank you."

The rest of the team rushed over, making sure they were okay. Denae checked a scrape on Leo's cheek. Mia hugged Emma while Vance bagged the axe. At least one of them was still focused on business. All Emma wanted to do was collapse and sleep through the weekend.

And hope Pastor Gregory Darl burned in Hell.

"I'm okay, I'm okay, Mia. Go help Vance. The faster we wrap up here, the faster I can go to bed."

Mia gave her a dimpled smile. "You did good."

Emma grinned back, then headed over to Julianna and helped her up. "Come with me, Mrs. Darl. You'll be taken into custody and processed by the sheriff's office." As Leo lifted Lizbet to her feet, Emma addressed her as well. "Same for you. You've both been very compliant so far. If we could continue that trend, Agent Ambrose and I would appreciate it."

Both Julianna and Lizbet seemed to have gone somewhere within themselves. Emma supposed this was a skill from years of abuse and being told to submit to evil men. She hoped their passivity served them well in prison.

When they reached the parking lot, Emma caught sight of Bo Somerson and Ian Darl. The two men rushed over, navigating the maze of haphazardly mixed sheriff vehicles and federal SUVs.

Emma waved over two deputies.

But Bo and Ian made it to her first. They wore identical looks of astonishment.

"Mom? It was you?"

Julianna offered a tired smile, as if she were a mother who'd been up all night with a toddler rather than a mother who'd been swinging an axe around all week. "Ian. You're safe. Your father won't hurt you anymore. All the children of Little Clementine are safe. Lead them well."

"What do you—"

"I'm sorry, Ian. Your father died. He was…pushed over the cliff's edge."

It was terrible to tell surviving family at the best of times, but standing there, holding his mother in handcuffs while she told him his father had just died, was about the worst moment Emma could imagine.

"Did you kill Dad, Mom?"

Julianna shook her head. She glanced over her shoulder at Lizbet.

"What?" It was Bo's turn to sound incredulous.

Lizbet also broke her silence, directing her words toward her husband. "Bo, please take care of the girls. I think I'll be gone for a while." Lizbet cast a glance at Ian and offered him an apologetic smile. "I may have taken your father, but I've left you my husband. Help him with the girls. They can be a handful."

Emma handed Julianna off to one of Sheriff Lowell's deputies, and Leo did likewise with Lizbet.

Together, Emma, Leo, Bo, and Ian watched the loaded cars drive away.

Ian turned toward Emma. "Do they really think they've accomplished something good here? They've murdered people."

Honesty seemed to be the only acceptable response to his inquiry. "People and emotions are complicated. I don't know why she didn't choose to report the crimes perpetrated against her, which seems like the obvious way to go to me. And I don't know why she didn't ask for outside help. But, hopefully, you," Emma smiled at him and Bo, "both of you, can be a healing force for your community. Though it will take some time to process."

"Amen."

40

Two days later, Emma was free of Little Clementine. Desperate to see a friendly face, she drove down to Richmond and met Keaton at The Lyft—a bar with a badass IPA selection.

Keaton's nose wrinkled as soon as the dark IPA hit his tongue, and Emma couldn't hold back a belly laugh. Her friend's lips pursed, his cheeks puffing out with the effort of making himself swallow, and he pushed the beer away before he found his voice.

For a moment, Emma thought he'd fall from their hightop table, he was so flustered.

"Not for you?"

Under the roving blue lights of the upscale bar, Keaton's pale skin practically looked aqua. He was one of a plentitude of sea creatures. Everybody looked like they were underwater in the mood lighting. And the gray stone floors might well have been the bottom of the ocean.

Emma pushed her Malibu Sunset cocktail Keaton's way and gestured for him to take a sip, which he did. "You're hilarious. How the hell did you go this long without trying an IPA?"

Her friend shook his head, scowling. "Wasn't long enough." He waved for their server's attention and pointed at Emma's drink.

Done with the beer, apparently.

Sitting there, Emma could almost pretend they were back on the job together, ribbing each other over drinks after a day at the office.

Sure, she was in nice jeans and a fluffy sweater that wouldn't have done her much good in the field, and Keaton wore a t-shirt and jeans instead of his normal suit, but this was comfortable. The Lyft had some history for their team too. It was where Winter Black had met Autumn Trent, way back when, before Emma had teamed up with them and dubbed their little group, partly in jest, the Super Squad.

That was a long time ago, but I wish it had lasted a little bit longer. Life in this job just has a way of bringing people together... and then forcing them apart.

Emma sipped her drink. "Well, at least they know how to make a decent fruity cocktail. I'm enjoying this so much, it's a good thing I'm not local."

Keaton shot a dirty look toward the offending beer. "It's Autumn's fault. Should've known she was punking me when she told me I'd love an IPA." He scrubbed his shaggy hair back from his face. "But, hey, she recommended this place too. Any complaints?"

"None yet." Emma bumped her glass against his fruity cocktail, celebrating the delivery of something he could actually enjoy.

Keaton sighed in exaggerated contentment after he ditched the straw and gulped down a bit of the drink. The roving blue lights overhead shifted across his face in a way that, just for a moment, made him appear a little ghoulish.

But he was just her best friend, no ghost. If only Emma could tell him everything.

I just wish he'd never left D.C.

"You miss me yet?" he asked, apparently reading her mind at least a little bit. No surprise there.

"You have no idea." She shook her head and picked up the cocktail menu, even though she had no real intention of ordering a different drink anytime soon. "Things are going fine, like I said, but I wish you and Neil hadn't left D.C. Hailey owes me one."

"Ha! For letting her big brother move down to take care of her? Somehow, I doubt she feels the same." Keaton grinned, his baby face looking even younger.

"She's good, though, you said?"

"Absolutely. Oh, you'll enjoy this story…"

Emma sat forward, relaxing into the familiar territory of Keaton's mad storytelling skills. Shy and nervous as he might be around strangers, her best friend had a way with words when he got to know a person, and the alcohol loosened up his lips until Emma thought she might know more about his kid sister's burgeoning career with the Richmond Police Department than Hailey herself did.

It was so good to see Keaton and celebrate his twenty-eighth birthday. Emma's whole body warmed to the occasion. Refreshed. Laughing again was also a very good thing.

Back in D.C., problems and questions only seemed to multiply even as cases kept getting solved. Like why the ghosts in the Other hated her and had barely spoken to her in Little Clementine. And why her mom's picture had gotten into the habit of falling down but been upright when Emma had returned home the day before…and remained that way when she'd woken up just that morning.

Laughing with Keaton was like taking a step back into the easier past, and exactly the therapeutic session she'd needed.

"...so Hailey tells the guy he can't have a crocodile as a pet...he lives in a downtown apartment, keep in mind. And you know what he does? He goes into a lecture on the differences between crocodiles and alligators, and then he tries to get her to sit down and watch some old Disney movie with dancing alligators, like she's going to suddenly change her mind and want to go get a six-foot lizard for herself. You believe that?"

Emma's laugh meshed with Keaton's, even as she followed his line of sight over to the upscale bar that spanned an entire wall of The Lyft. Two bartenders were on duty, one of them being Autumn's sister, Sarah Nichol, who'd just recently started working there. Emma leaned in toward her friend, keeping her eyes on his telltale cheeks. "I see Sarah's here tonight."

Sure enough, he blushed, jarring a little in his seat as his focus came back to her. "Uh, yeah. She makes a mean drink." He wrapped his hand around his cocktail and took a long drink, only to glance back at the bar again. "And she's pretty special."

For a moment, Emma felt guilty about enjoying a night out like this. Oren Werling's face appeared in her mind, along with his constant offers of another yoga session. She'd only taken the one class so far, but it had been an...experience. One she wouldn't mind repeating at least once. Maybe more than once.

Why was she thinking about Oren and his yoga studio at a time like this?

She was out with her best friend, raising a toast to his birthday and watching him get googly-eyed at the woman behind the bar.

Emma followed her friend's gaze to the confident blond wiping down the counter and sweeping up glasses.

Busy, smiling, chatty...Sarah looked healthy and happy.

Emma leaned in and knocked her drink against his to grab his attention once more.

A smile crept along her face, betraying her suspicions early. "How special is she?"

Keaton's cheeks turned beet red—well, purple—under the blue lights. "She's Autumn's sister. We're just here to... support her. Say hi later when, uh, the bar is less busy."

Emma grinned. "Okay, birthday boy, whatever you say."

Besties always know. No getting around that, friend.

41

Leo played his fingers along the red-and-white checkered tablecloth, fighting down nerves. He shouldn't be nervous…right? He and Denae weren't on a date. Not exactly anyway.

I just asked her if she wanted to grab a slice or two. Maybe a drink.

On a Saturday night.

Maybe that was it? Saturday night, they hadn't been on the job all day…yet they were spending the evening together.

And he'd put on cologne, too, after telling himself he wouldn't.

Denae smiled from across the table, her eyes crinkling like she could tell exactly what he was thinking in the busy little pizzeria. She was dressed in a cute little navy-blue dress —very different from her work attire. There was even smoky eyeliner around her dark-brown eyes. Her natural hair curled around her face, accentuating her fine bone structure.

Looks like a date, sounds like a date, feels like a date, smells like a date…

Fuck it. It's a date.

He coughed, fighting down the buzzing nerves in his stomach.

The server delivered beers and promised their pie would be up shortly. Whatever "shortly" meant on a Saturday night in downtown D.C. When she left, Leo turned his attention back to Denae. "Why am I nervous?"

Denae laughed, emotion darkening her cheeks as he shook his head. "You are?"

"I did not mean to say that out loud."

"I could tell." She leaned forward, reminding him that the scoop-neck dress she wore was very much not a buttoned-up blouse she'd wear in the office. Not nearly risqué...but not very FBI-agent either. "But, hey, the feeling's mutual, okay? We're finally getting a chance to get to know each other outside work. There are no murderers to chase or keep us up all night."

He chuckled, leaning back in his chair and attempting to relax. "Yeah, you asked me earlier what I think of D.C. Honestly, I don't know yet, as far as the city goes, because I've been working nonstop since I got here. When I'm not working, I've been busy with all the logistical stuff that goes along with a move...you know. Unpacking, getting bills moved over, truck registration transferred. All that adulting mess."

Denae smoothed some of her curls down over her ear, nodding along. "And how about the work? You settling in with the team? Trust me, I know it can be awkward coming onto a team where some of us have worked together for a while. Like the new kid at school. Mia might be new to the team, but she's not new to Emma and Vance and me."

The server dropped by with fresh garlic knots, and Leo picked one up and took a bite. Fresh, warm...comfortable. Like the same appetizer would've been at his favorite pizza place in Miami, in fact. He might regret eating too much garlic later, though.

"It helps to have Jacinda here." He chewed thoughtfully. "But I like the team. I'm glad I came. I think Agent Last might be warming up to me a little. She was a tad skittish at first."

He chuckled, popping the rest of the knot into his mouth as Denae bit into one across from him.

"Meh, don't take Emma too personally." She shrugged, licking her lips to pull in some of the extra garlic butter she'd missed. "Emma's best friend, Keaton Holland, moved to Richmond right before you and Jacinda came. Not having him on the team was already a big loss. Then a new boss…it's a tough transition. New faces replacing favorite old ones, you know? Besides, you two seem to work well together."

"Yeah, that all makes sense." And knowing that had been comforting too…if not exactly helpful in terms of honing their dynamic as a team. "Just been a long time since I've been the new kid on the playground."

Denae smiled, most of her hard edges oozing away with the beer. "Well, hey, I kinda like the new kid. He knows his pizza anyway." She gestured her approval with a garlic knot, pursing her lips. "And that's kind of how the FBI works when it comes to agent transfers, right? They get thrown to the wolves."

Leo choked on his garlic knot, jerking in his chair. His esophagus burned with a violent coughing fit as his eyes watered and colors blurred before him.

Denae pushed his water toward him until he'd taken the glass. He forced down one sip, then another, getting rid of the now-tasteless bread.

Wolves. Dang wolves again.

"You okay?"

Around them, diners at other tables stared, assessing

whether someone needed to perform a Heimlich. He waved off the concerned expressions, willing his breath to even out.

Across from him, Denae sat, eyes wide, with her fingers splayed on the table as if she were going to leap up and bear-hug him from behind.

Finally, he managed to speak again. "Fine…I'm fine. Just…just went down the wrong way."

Denae's lips were parted, and a tiny line creased between her eyebrows. She leaned across the table and rested one hand on his forearm, waiting for him to meet her eyes before she spoke. "Was it something I said?"

42

Emma coasted her Prius past the park bordering Keaton's neighborhood, admiring the greenery that was surviving the winter. Her windows open to the chilly air, she took a deep breath to help wake herself up and perhaps fight back the slight hangover lurking at the back of her skull.

She'd left Keaton's reluctantly before breakfast was even discussed, refusing his invitation to lie around his couch or guest room for a while.

He'd been headed out the door to meet his sister for some family time anyway.

Might as well get going...get home, eat, and maybe take an afternoon nap too. Keaton's guest room bed was fine but was nothing compared to her luxury mattress.

Her best friend had shown no sign of a hangover, which she'd found interesting. Perhaps that meant he was finding his way to The Lyft—and Sarah Nichol—more often than he'd let on?

Considering how rarely I've got the time and luxury to drink,

I'm lucky I'm not passed out on a floor. Four drinks...what was I thinking? Thank goodness I drank a few glasses of water too.

Emma slid into the turn lane that would take her toward the Richmond Field Office. Even if her reasons were bittersweet and sentimental, she wanted to see the place again while in town. The office would be mostly abandoned on a quiet Sunday morning, so there'd be no risk of having to explain her presence.

She rolled her window up against the cold and sipped at the hot coffee Keaton had poured her. Emma debated whether to stop and walk around once she reached the office or just cruise by and get on her way to D.C.

Delaying her trip wouldn't do her any good, would it? She'd still be leaving Keaton behind all over again.

Taking the turnoff for the FBI complex, Emma slowed down, thinking about when she'd last been there. It was when she'd helped Keaton move down and get settled, or so she thought.

Then her eye caught a form way down on the sidewalk.

The figure was coming toward her. Fast. Too fast to be human.

With it came a fierce, cold wind she felt through the Prius's vents.

Emma swerved to the side of the road and hit the brake just as the figure arrived.

He's got no head. He's got no fucking head.

The specter darted in front of her car and came around to her driver's side window, wearing khakis and a bloody polo. Blood streaked his arms and hands, but the lack of a head made her stammer.

When the figure crouched beside her, bloody fingers poking into the car through the crack of her barely lowered window, Emma saw that the ghost did have a face. A glowing, transparent, phantom head sat atop his shoulders.

Whited-out eyes peered at her, and Emma fought the urge to hit the gas and flee as fast as she could.

She resisted and gripped the steering wheel, forcing herself to face the ghost. That was the least she could do. Whatever this poor soul had been through, the event had left him without a head. Seemed to be a theme. Given her abilities and her line of work, it wouldn't be fair of her to deny his presence, his fate, and run away.

She still couldn't make herself roll down her window any farther, though, but that made no difference.

The ghost's bloodied, phantom half face leaned toward her. Straight through the glass in a way that made her lean sideways, straining against her seat belt to give the apparition space.

"You have to help me find my sister." Its voice echoed in the still air of the Prius. "Her name is Mia. I don't understand where she's gone."

Emma opened her mouth but found no words.

Ned Logan had lost his sister…and found Emma instead.

The End
To be continued…

Thank you for reading.
All of the Emma Last Series books can be found on Amazon.

ACKNOWLEDGMENTS

How does one properly thank everyone involved in taking a dream and making it a reality? Let me try.

In addition to my family, whose unending support provided the foundation for me to find the time and energy to put these thoughts on paper, I want to thank the editors who polished my words and made them shine.

Many thanks to my publisher for risking taking on a newbie and giving me the confidence to become a bona fide author.

More than anyone, I want to thank you, my reader, for clicking on a nobody and sharing your most important asset, your time, with this book. I hope with all my heart I made it worthwhile.

Much love,
  Mary

ABOUT THE AUTHOR

Mary Stone lives among the majestic Blue Ridge Mountains of East Tennessee with her two dogs, four cats, a couple of energetic boys, and a very patient husband.

As a young girl, she would go to bed every night, wondering what type of creature might be lurking underneath. It wasn't until she was older that she learned that the creatures she needed to most fear were human.

Today, she creates vivid stories with courageous, strong heroines and dastardly villains. She invites you to enter her world of serial killers, FBI agents but never damsels in distress. Her female characters can handle themselves, going toe-to-toe with any male character, protagonist or antagonist.

Discover more about Mary Stone on her website.
www.authormarystone.com

- facebook.com/authormarystone
- twitter.com/MaryStoneAuthor
- goodreads.com/AuthorMaryStone
- bookbub.com/profile/3378576590
- pinterest.com/MaryStoneAuthor
- instagram.com/marystoneauthor
- tiktok.com/@authormarystone